The Rainforest

Latin American Women Writers

Alicia Steimberg

The Rainforest

❦ La selva

Translated and with
an introduction by
Andrea G. Labinger

University of Nebraska Press
Lincoln and London

Publication of this book was assisted by a grant from
the National Endowment for the Arts 🌱

© Alicia Steimberg, 2000. Published by arrangement
with Julie Popkin, Literary Agent, 15340 Albright St.,
#204, Pacific Palisades CA 90272.

Translation © 2006 by the Board of Regents of the
University of Nebraska. All rights reserved. Manu-
factured in the United States of America.

    ⊚

Book typeset and designed by Richard Eckersley in
Adobe Minion and Enschedé Trinité fonts.

Library of Congress Cataloging-in-Publication Data
Steimberg, Alicia, 1933–
[Selva English]
The rainforest = La selva / Alicia Steimberg ; trans-
lated with an introduction by Andrea G. Labinger.
p. cm. –   (Latin American women writers)
Cover title: Selva.
ISBN-13: 978-0-8032-4315-6 (cloth: alkaline paper)
ISBN-10 : 0-8032-4315-4 (cloth: alkaline paper)
ISBN-13: 978-0-8032-9329-8 (paperback: alkaline paper)
ISBN-10: 0-8032-9329-1 (paperback: alkaline paper)
I. Title: Selva.   II. Labinger, Andrea G.   III. Title.
IV. Series.
PQ7798.29.T36S4513 2006   863'.64–dc22   2005032152

Andrea G. Labinger

Introduction

At first glance, *The Rainforest* (*La selva*) would appear to be Argentine author Alicia Steimberg's most conventional narrative to date. Cecilia, a woman on the threshold of her sixties, arrives at a Brazilian rainforest spa in the hope that the gentle climate and attentive staff will help her heal her profound psychological wounds and escape her daily preoccupations. In this unlikely place, Cecilia meets and falls in love with Steve, a North American who has come to the spa in search of serenity after having suffered traumas not unlike Cecilia's own. But not even a new romance can eclipse Cecilia's anguished past, as her memory frequently drifts back to Dardo, her deceased husband, and to Federico, their wayward son, while Steve battles fears and demons of his own. Mutual discovery is a constant source of both joy and consternation for the lovers. Cecilia, for example, is greatly surprised to learn that Steve practices hang gliding, and even reluctantly agrees to accompany him on a flight, clearly a metaphor for Cecilia's healing process as she slowly learns to overcome her many fears. In effect, danger and security are subtly recurrent themes in this mature novel, with the benevolent rainforest symbolically representing an oasis of controlled excitement and carefully choreographed leaps of faith.

Largely absent from this apparently simple tale of love, anguish, and redemption are Steimberg's characteristically surreal digressions, her multiple narrative points of view, and her often hilarious disquisitions on the idiosyncrasies of language. Yet, a closer reading reveals that *The Rainforest* is, indeed, vintage Steimberg, offering the reader an array of intelligently nuanced characters, a concern with transcendence, and Steimberg's typical, well-honed sense of the absurd. Witness, for example, Cecilia's rumination on ants:

There they go, marching in long rows, always so disciplined, each one carrying its little leaf or petal. I don't admire or torture them any more, as I did when I was a kid, but sometimes, since I have nothing else to do with my time, I get the urge. To pick up an ant and place it way back at the end of the line, ever so carefully. How would I feel if an enormous hand were to lift me up and deposit me at the end of the line at the bank or the post office?

That enormous hand belongs, of course, to the deity in whom Steimberg sometimes believes and sometimes doesn't, a conundrum that has infused her work ever since her first novel, *Músicos y relojeros*, was published by Centro Editor de América Latina in 1971, with three subsequent editions. Praised by *Publisher's Weekly* as "small gem," *Músicos y relojeros* was a finalist in two literary competitions – Barcelona's Barral and Monte Ávila in Caracas – that same year. Translated as *Musicians and Watchmakers* (Latin American Literary Review Press, 1998), the novel describes the vicissitudes of a Jewish girl's fractured childhood in Catholic, Peronist Argentina, and the conflicts engendered by the two warring branches of her family, one of which exhorts her to be proud of her heritage while the other warns her to keep silent or, at most, to "say you're nothing," when asked about her background. Because of its eloquent articulation of the question of mixed identity, *Musicians and Watchmakers*, a truly multiethnic *Bildungsroman*, has come to occupy an important place in the growing canon of Latin American Jewish studies.

With her second novel, *La loca 101* (*Madwoman 911*, 1973), Steimberg introduces the experimental technique that has come to be appreciated as a hallmark of her style. Through a collage of typical *porteño* characters, *La loca 101* explores the theme of sanity – a staple in Steimberg's oeuvre – while providing a satirical commentary on the psychoanalytic mania that consumed middle-class Argentines in the 1970s. Not coincidentally, *La loca 101* also establishes a courageous analogy between her protagonist's mental illness and the national insanity that gripped Argentina during that decade. Steimberg returns to the theme of emotional instability in *El árbol del placer* (*The Pleasure Tree*, 1986), where the subject is given a more sardonic treatment, this time without political overtones.

Further psychological and ontological explorations can be found in Steimberg's third novel, the critically underexamined, but none-theless compelling, *Su espíritu inocente* (*Innocent Spirit*, 1981), a continuation of the story begun in *Musicians and Watchmakers*, now projected into a tumultuous adolescence with its concomitant concerns: sexual awakening, the formation and dissolution of rela-tionships, and, underlying it all, constant doubts about God's role in determining human happiness. Technically more sophisticated than *Musicians and Watchmakers* – and just as outrageous – *Inno-cent Spirit* introduces a fragmented, postmodern style that even-tually culminates in *Cuando digo Magdalena* (Planeta 1992; *Call Me Magdalena*, trans. Andrea G. Labinger, University of Nebraska Press, 2002), winner of the prestigious Planeta Prize and arguably Steimberg's literary *tour de force*. British scholar Shelley Godsland has described *Magdalena* as an "anti-detective novel," comparing it to Auster's *City of Glass* for its "preoccupation with the function of language" (*Bulletin of Hispanic Studies*, October 2002). Godsland is correct in observing that while *Magdalena* may be framed as a sus-pense novel, its true enigma resides in its exploration of human identity and polysemy. Set on a ranch on the outskirts of Buenos Aires, this loosely structured, ostensible murder mystery is really a backdrop for a more compelling drama: the psychological profile of Magdalena, an insecure, emotionally fragile woman whose fre-quent name changes reflect her volatility. The plot of *Magdalena* is equally unpredictable. Like a sequence of riffs on a familiar jazz tune, *Call Me Magdalena* follows a number of seemingly disparate themes which ultimately come together, leading the reader through the vagaries of Magdalena's Argentine Jewish childhood, almost certainly one of the roots of her perpetual angst.

It should be pointed out that Magdalena can be seen as a precur-sor of *The Rainforest*'s Cecilia. Both women have endured devastat-ing psychological blows (Magdalena's are unspecified, while Cecilia's are thoroughly documented); both withdraw physically in search of solace (Magdalena goes to a ranch, accompanied by mem-bers of her mind control class, while Cecilia accepts her friends' generous offer to pay for a rainforest spa retreat); both tread on emotionally precarious terrain. Yet, Cecilia is by far the stronger character. Unlike the disoriented Magdalena – and, indeed, unlike other, earlier Steimberg protagonists – Cecilia never loses sight of who she is or where she comes from. While she may rely on a compass to help her navigate the sinuous path leading from her hotel room to the rainforest and back again, she always manages to find her way home, physically, psychologically, and spiritually. It might be argued that Cecilia is a traditional *petite bourgeoise*, the inevitable product of a generation of women who were taught that happiness and security depend on the presence of a man in their lives. And the dashing Steve – whether dancing romantically to fifties tunes, floating through the air on his hang glider, or solicitously helping Cecilia with the dishes – certainly fills anyone's definition of the Modern Maturity version of Prince Charming. Yet, this prince's charms pale in comparison to the masterful portrayal of Cecilia's unexpected strength as she engages in one daily struggle after another: caring for the dying Dardo, confronting her son's drug-induced rages, protecting herself from domestic violence, and, ultimately, allowing herself to feel again.

Steimberg is also the author of *Amatista* (1989), an award-winning, tongue-in-cheek erotic novel about lust and language; two collections of short stories: *Como todas las mañanas* (*Just Like Every Morning*, 1983) and *Vidas y vueltas* (*The Conversation of the Saints and Other Stories*, 1999); and two adolescent novellas with recipes: *El mundo no es de polenta* (*The World Isn't Made of Polenta*, 1991) and *Una tarde de invierno un submarino* (*Hot Chocolate Afternoon*, 2001). Steimberg's work has been extensively translated and anthologized. An accomplished translator and teacher herself, Steimberg is currently working on a guide for aspiring writers, *Aprender a escribir* (*Learning to Write*).

The Rainforest

I'm in the rainforest, and it's very hot and humid; at times a warm drizzle falls. Eyes closed, I lift my face to catch the water and drink a little, while a steel-blue and cadmium-yellow macaw watches me without turning its head. This is how I spend my days, among charming monkeys, benevolent serpents, motionless parrots, and foliage that enfolds me. With each step I take, flower-laden branches envelop me. I'd gladly remain here, tasting raindrops and picking the occasional fruit from the lowest branches. The fruit resembles chirimoyas, mangos, bananas.

There's no danger of getting lost in the rainforest. My compass guides me whenever it's time to return. I know I have to head east, and in fifteen minutes I'm in the clearing where the hotel is located. As you approach the hotel in the afternoon, you can smell dinner: there's always rice with vegetables and meat, poultry, or seafood, everything seasoned with fragrant herbs. They raise the fowl in a chicken coop out back. I love to go in there and steal a freshly laid egg for the next morning's breakfast. The chickens here don't get a balanced diet, just natural food, so they have that marvelous, old-fashioned flavor and aroma. It reminds me of an educational poster I always used to look for in the library of the teacher's college when I was studying for my degree. The poster was old and worn: it almost certainly dated back to the nineteenth century when the school was founded, and I used it for a demonstration lesson for an elementary school class. It showed some multicolored chickens and a magnificent rooster, illuminated by a sunbeam streaming across a wire fence. In those hectic, tense years of my youth, when it frightened me to realize that I didn't know what I wanted (I'm practically an old woman now, and I'm still not sure), that chicken coop picture was like a refuge. As a girl, I used to get sick quite often, and Mama was convinced that the country, with its fresh air, was the key to good health. After coming down with measles (regular and German), tonsillitis, and various forms of flu, they brought me to a house with a chicken coop like this one (I don't know where it was

– kids follow their parents just as chicks trot after hens – all I know is that we used to travel by train to a sunny little town where the house was). There I would faithfully spy through the wire fence on the birds, their chicks, and their eggs, their perennial reproduction of life.

The place where I am now is, to be precise, a convalescent facility, although no one uses that term to describe it. They simply call it "the spa." After a whole day of long walks in the rainforest, I appreciate what I see when I return to the hotel: rough-hewn furniture, a large mirror with a moth-specked frame, the tables in the little dining room, my room and my bed. The recommendation is to sleep on a mattress on the floor, Japanese-style, but that strikes me as a bit too ascetic. I sleep soundly in the bed and awaken to the singing of birds and the fragrance of honeysuckle. I thought I'd have to wear high boots in order to avoid mosquito bites, but none of that's necessary because this is a safe rainforest. There are ants, true, but I suppose they have some ecological purpose. There they go, marching in long rows, always so disciplined, each one carrying its little leaf or petal. I don't admire or torture them anymore, as I did when I was a kid, but sometimes, since I have nothing else to do with my time, I get the urge to pick up an ant and place it way back at the end of the line, ever so carefully. How would I feel if an enormous hand were to lift me up and deposit me at the end of the line at the bank or the post office? I think loneliness and the warm, humid, slightly enervating climate that always makes me feel like I'm about to fall asleep are responsible for these silly ideas. When I go back to the hotel at sunset, I sink into a wooden tub full of warm water strewn with huge flower petals.

I wear low-necked dresses, loose and comfortable, because of the heat, which is constant. I've learned to perspire without feeling grubby. I have breakfast and dinner at the hotel without exchanging a word with a group of pale Finns who occupy the other tables. I don't understand the language of the locals – dark-skinned, dark-haired people with black, black eyes, and I don't understand Finnish, either. The friends who recommended this place to me told me about the Finns: they come here for reasons like mine; only they don't suffer from confusion but, rather, from a suicidal sadness that descends on them from the cold and the leaden sky they have to endure in their country ten months of the year.

I glance at my watch: six p.m. Leaves and flowers brush my arms, and my tears mingle with the raindrops that have begun to fall. I cry and feel better. I can't see the sky, just the tops of the tall trees and a monkey swinging from a branch. What I wouldn't give right now to be alone on a sultry afternoon, with a storm threatening, at the Buenos Aires Zoo, breathing in the scent of the animals by an algae-covered lake. I lie down on a bed of leaves at the foot of a colossal tree and fall asleep. When I awaken, I see that it's grown dark enough to start back. When a little light filters through the branches, I realize I'm close to the clearing. Before leaving my solitude behind, I let out a scream that's like a howl.

Evening. A bath in the wooden tub in my room. The Ambrée soap that I bought at the duty-free shop lies on a wicker chair next to the tub, where they've also left a good, rough towel. I've taken off my dress and underwear and thrown them on the mosaic tile floor. At home I wouldn't tolerate those crumpled, rain-soaked garments piled up on the floor for even one minute, but here I've succumbed to indolence. Anyway, there's always someone around to take care of my things. When I get back to this room after dinner, they'll have picked it all up, and everything will be in order: the bed turned down, an After Eight mint on the pillow, like a talisman against barbarism.

After I dry myself off, I toss the used towel on the floor with the rest of the stuff and dress for dinner in clothing that's been impeccably washed and ironed by the hotel staff. A dress very similar to the one I took off, only a different color. My daily wardrobe consists of six short, loose dresses in pastel shades: Nile green, old rose, light blue, cream, chalk white, cerise. Sleeveless, square-necked. A few pair of flimsy sandals, or else I go barefoot. I use only citrus fragrances; it's impossible to consider heavier perfumes in this constant heat. I've arranged my cosmetics, combs, and brushes on the unfinished wooden stand in the bathroom.

My table in the dining room is next to a large window through which you can see only the garden, with its ancient palm trees. I like that: my long daily walk among leafy trees is sufficient for me. At each table there's always a basket overflowing with fruit; the recommendation is to eat at least two pieces of fruit before the rice dish. The fruits resemble those we're familiar with, but, like the chickens, they're larger and tastier. I choose something that looks like a banana, and a fruit that's like a kiwi but twice the size. A delicious combination. The Finns are still pale and serious, hardly exchanging a word among themselves, and it's already been almost four weeks. I guess they don't go down to the beach because they're afraid of skin cancer. Mostly, none of them looks at me, but today I discovered one of them staring at me with curiosity. Curiosity, and something like passion. He glanced away quickly, coughing a little and covering his mouth with his hand.

By crossing a different part of the rainforest, you can reach the sea, a beach called San Conrado. In order to get there very early, the only time of day when the heat is bearable, you have to leave at dawn. I picked up all this information in Buenos Aires. At the agency specializing in non-touristy spas, the same agency that brought me to this place (a weekly flight from Rio to a neighboring town and from there a helicopter that arrives daily with new guests, mail, and provisions), they explained that as far back as anyone can remember, no one has ever ventured into the rainforest at night, so they can't describe what goes on there. Do the animals go wild at night? I stare at the people at the other tables, and then I discover a man who isn't Finnish. He's sort of blond, but not as blond as they are, athletic build, graying at the temples, blue eyes, and pleasantly tanned skin, lined with the requisite wrinkles (what would I do with a face as smooth as a magnolia?). He's looking at me, too. He's been waiting patiently for me to discover him, his fork poised in midair. When I glance his way at last, he smiles and nods his head, picks up his silverware, plates, and his fruit cup, and moves over to my table. He's a North American, from California; surrounded by so many unapproachable Scandinavians and mysterious natives, we feel a kinship, like a meeting of old friends.

Steve speaks spiritedly, half in Spanish and half in English. He tells me he's a biologist, he does research, he travels a lot, and he's lived in Mexico. Tonight the rice dish is especially tasty, and Steve has brought over a bottle of wine from his table. The dessert is the most delicate orange mousse I've ever tasted, and I smile to think how effortlessly both he and I consume sophisticated wines and desserts in such an apparently primitive place; we realize that the rustic ambience has been carefully orchestrated. After dinner the same helicopter that brought us the orange mousse and the seafood for the rice will carry us over the rainforest to the beach, ringed with twenty-story hotels with revolving cafés. On the top floor of the

tallest building, Steve and I have our first drink together and dance
to old songs.

It only happens
When I dance with you

And I notice that every curve and hollow of my body fits tenderly
into the contours of this man I've just met.

When weather conditions are ideal, they say, in the very early
morning and at nightfall, the hang gliders launch themselves from
the terrace of the twentieth floor.

When I arrived at the rainforest spa, I didn't realize I was going to think so often of Dardo. He's been gone eight years already, eleven months after the fatal diagnosis. During those months, contrary to what I had anticipated, he suffered no extreme pain that couldn't be relieved with drugs, but he became more and more incapacitated, as his doctor had predicted. One year's survival, he said. Dardo was hospitalized for an entire month so that, by using new, sophisticated technology, they might find the microscopic primary tumor that had caused the metastasis to his bones. But the cancer was very advanced, and there was no cure, the oncologist said. He told me first, during a conversation we had while Dardo was in the hospital.

The oncologist was a well-dressed, fat man. I never saw him in a white coat.

"You have a tumor," he told him a few days after the conversation with me. Dardo and the doctor treated each other as equals. They were two professionals: an engineer and a physician.

Dardo received the news with a smile: the meaning hadn't registered. They had dulled his pain with analgesics, and his color was good: that day he had eaten his lunch eagerly; he seemed very calm, even happy. Happiness can also come from the disappearance of pain.

"I'm very glad to be in this hospital," he said. "I feel very well cared for."

The doctor smiled, and I smiled, too.

"Now we're going to find out where the tumor is – that's why we're putting you in the hospital," the doctor continued, "to locate the tumor."

There was no reply. Dardo turned his head, calmly looking at a treetop through the window.

Dardo had had two accidents in a row, one involving his hip and the other his arm. The orthopedists dealt with him as orthopedists do, and our family physician's intervention was necessary in order to send him to another specialist who would investigate more carefully and interpret the X-rays correctly.

The first accident took place in Buenos Aires. After a fall Dardo started to feel a pain in his hip that wouldn't go away, but he insisted on continuing to work, overcome by pain and taking a ton of medications.

I went on a business trip for a week. When I returned, I was surprised to find Dardo at home. Opening the door to the apartment, I saw him sitting in a chair, smiling broadly at the other end of the living room, surrounded by people: his mother; Sebastián and Federico, my older boys; and two friends who had stopped by to visit. He didn't get up to greet me, but at that moment I was aware only of his unexpected presence at home at eleven o'clock in the morning; it took me a few more seconds to realize why he hadn't stood up to meet me: his right arm was in a sling. There had been another "accident": he had been mugged while crossing the street. They had knocked him to the ground, grabbed his briefcase, and left him at the mercy of the oncoming cars as the light turned green. Some passersby managed to spot him. Traffic stopped, an ambulance arrived; he was taken to a hospital, where a cast was applied to his broken right arm. Dardo hadn't wanted to disrupt my trip or frighten me, so when he saw me come in, he smiled and smiled; he explained, everyone explained. The next day the pain was so unbearable that he decided to go to another clinic, where they determined that the cast was on wrong, and they reset the arm in a different position.

In the X-rays both parts of his fractured humerus appeared like two veal bones placed randomly on a butcher counter. Once the break was reduced, the two sections looked more aligned, but there was still a little space between them.

The bone didn't heal as quickly as expected. The orthopedists changed the cast a few more times, varying the position of the arm. Dardo suffered from severe pain in his arm and hip; he took powerful painkillers, he slept a lot. Weeks later the X-rays showed that his fracture still hadn't healed.

Finally, they took off the cast, replacing it with a bandage. Dardo took sick leave from his job; I continued working. The household functioned as usual. Every morning the cleaning woman turned it into a pleasant, orderly place smelling of floor wax and the good food she prepared and left for us. As Dardo's pain continued, the new orthopedic specialist recommended by the clinic ordered a CT scan that revealed the cause of the problem: a primary tumor of unknown origin had metastasized to the bone. The most agonizing thing wasn't so much the time lost in useless treatments but the fact that the cancer was quite advanced and now nothing could save Dardo from pain and death.

Me, Cecilia, hang gliding? There's something about Steve that convinces me immediately that anything he suggests is all right. These flying devices are simple and apparently very safe – in fact, as safe as airplanes. There are thousands of flights every day, and people travel as calmly as if they were on a bus. Once in a while, in a very great while, one falls down. It must be that famous exception that proves the rule, although I never did understand why an exception had to prove a rule. In San Conrado, at least, I never heard anyone say there had been an accident. So, without knowing quite how, one morning I found myself seated and firmly secured in a contraption designed for two people, with Steve at my side commanding the controls that could change the flight's direction.

This is a sport that depends totally on weather conditions, like flying a glider. Flight instructors for gliders, just like flight instructors for hang gliders, are weather experts. At the lecture given by the San Conrado instructor, I learned which clouds predicted rain, which ones meant wind, which ones simply a cold front. In any event I didn't have to do anything, just sit next to Steve, well protected by seat belts, and launch myself into the void alongside him.

As we took the elevator up to the top floor of the café, I was seized by terror, but the same thing happens to me whenever I have to get on a plane: I'm frightened beforehand, but when I'm in the air, I'm never afraid. I wasn't even scared when they made us stand on a parapet on the unrailed terrace – which you could reach as soon as a guard opened the imposing iron gates – and the technicians activated the machine and set it in place. I can't recall the moment when they launched us into the air. I only felt, to my great relief, that, instead of falling, we were rising. The wings inflated; the air carried us upward. Steve was at the controls, and I recovered just enough to look around as we flew over the beach. It was a glorious day, not a single cloud; the greenish blue of the sea was punctuated by many-colored ships and the sunbathers' umbrellas on the beach.

The only thing that frightened me a little was my own elation. I had felt this way in Spain, when I arrived at El Escorial with a group of friends during a snowstorm, and as we walked into a bar filled with heat and light, they gave each of us a cup of hot chocolate laced with cognac. I felt the blood rushing through my veins like a torrent. In normal situations nobody feels their own blood, and yet blood flows all the time. At that moment I felt it coursing downward in strong waves from my head to my feet, and it was also something like understanding, even vaguely, why some people believe in God. You never see your own blood rushing through your veins, I thought, and yet it flows, it flows all the time along with your life.

In the distance you could see other hang gliders in full flight. Only then did I dare turn my head a little to look at Steve, and I noticed him looking at me, smiling, his eyes slightly misty. Now we were flying in large circles along the shoreline, going down, down, until we landed gently on the pure white sand, a judicious distance away from the sunbathers and their umbrellas.

Everything is so quick and easy with Steve – it seems like a bonus provided by the spa. But Steve is a convalescent tourist like me. There are no young patients here. No one is physically ill, either, if one can distinguish between physical ailments and sickness of the soul; however, they haven't cut out the medication I've been taking lately, these little pink pills that I consider a protective wall around me and my upheavals. Undeniably, chemistry, along with psychology and psychoanalysis, has made great advances. The people here are, as they say, "middle-aged," and as everyone knows, middle age seems to come along later and later in life. No young people would think of looking for a place like this to recover in; they couldn't afford it. I can't afford it myself: two old friends took it upon themselves to find this spa and take care of the bills, and they'll continue to do so for as long as necessary. Recovery time varies, from a few weeks up to an entire year, but the long-term residents' routine changes. In the little hotel bar, where one can hear the voices of Jacques Brel and Nina Simone (there's a version of *Ne me quitte pas* by each of them), I feel stronger and healthier than ever.

In Buenos Aires I've seen youngsters smile tenderly at older people ("that old couple," they say) embracing. I couldn't stand that kind of tenderness. Yes, we do have wrinkles, but Steve is athletic, and I dye my hair with dark-blonde henna. An Irish song I learned when I was twenty starts off like this:

Darling, I am growing old,
Silver threads among the gold,
But, my darling, you will be,
Always young and fair to me.

I embrace Steve, and he presses me against his chest.

Today I went out at the usual time, and a little while later I found myself in the middle of the rainforest. The branches scraped my arms, and the heat and humidity intensified. I kept going, as usual, without a fixed destination, because the flora and fauna are always the same, and it doesn't matter whether you go in one direction or another, but this time I came upon some extremely worn, stone steps. I climbed down twenty steps, where the air was even hotter and more humid, the vegetation thicker, and I felt a bit weary. Thirty steps later (I counted them for lack of anything better to do) my legs were shaking, and I had to sit down. It's odd: I always thought people got tired going upstairs, not down. I reached a precarious bridge that spanned a stream. My body gradually became accustomed to the new atmospheric conditions, and I began walking along a path at the water's edge. As I rounded the bend, my gaze fell upon a pleasant waterfall. It didn't look anything like the roaring falls of Iguazú; it was small and merry, like a shower. Without thinking twice, I took off my dress and sandals, leaving them next to my purse with the compass in it, and plunged my feet into the water. Gratefully, I noticed it was cooler than the rainwater, and so, splashed by the falling rain and by the water I kicked up from the rocks at the bottom, I headed toward the little waterfall. No crocodiles, no *yacarés*. Then I lay down on the grass beneath a majestic tree and fell into a sweet slumber with those disconnected thoughts that come just before sleep. I thought of Steve.

Steve's routine here is very different from mine. Here no one forces anyone to do anything; instead, they give you options to choose from. Steve doesn't walk in the rainforest, but he's fervently devoted to hang gliding, which I gave up after that first attempt. But we both choose to eat and sleep together.

Sometimes, like now, Steve turns over and falls asleep; I embrace his body and fall asleep, too. Other times I settle at his side without disentangling my legs from his, and I grab a book. I can tell already that I won't sleep tonight – I'm too edgy and wide awake. In about two hours Steve will wake up, think I'm sleeping, and place a delicate kiss on my forehead before going down to the beach. I'll open my eyes for one second and then fall back into my lethargy. If I can't sleep tonight, I'll sleep on my walk through the rainforest, on the bed of leaves at the foot of my tree next to the waterfall.

Old Time is still a-flying,
And this same flower that blooms today,
Tomorrow will be dying.

Robert Herrick says it with a certain annoyance, because four hundred years ago people made him get up from his tomb to repeat these words. Yes, it's true: tonight I drank a bit more than my usual glass of wine.

My compass guides me to the stream and waterfall: I need to continue north for about ten more minutes to find the staircase. Now that I'm used to it, I find climbing down pleasant. I take a dip in the waterfall, then stretch out on a bed of leaves, always beneath the same tree. I fall asleep, and I dream, and I remember my dreams. This afternoon I dreamed I was at my birthday party, and all the guests started to describe their dreams. A dream where people describe their dreams. My friends described very serious, melancholy, and even philosophical dreams.

I said: "Last night I dreamed I was at my birthday party. I got up to go to the bathroom, sat down on the toilet seat, and peed on the lid. There was no bathroom door, and some guests I didn't even know were watching."

In my dream, after I said this, there was a disapproving silence, and then I got up and brought in the cake with the little candles. Everyone applauded, sang, and took pictures. I blew out the candles. A heavy rain woke me from both dreams.

In the rainforest the rain never forces you to go back to the hotel before you plan to. As the thick drops stream down my body, I notice that my dress, draped over a low branch, has become a sodden rag. I lie down again, but the water falling in my face keeps me from sleeping. Then I slip on the dripping dress, pick up the waterproof, tightly sealed purse where I keep my compass, and start walking.

We live and die without ever seeing the inside of our bodies. Not too long ago, a friend's five-year-old grandson saw a skeleton, and they told him he had one just like that inside him; they even made him feel the hardness of his own little bones in his shoulders, his head, his ankles . . . This made an impression on the poor child that lasted several days. It was useless to reassure him that it's good we have a skeleton to hold us up and keep us from collapsing to the ground like rag dolls. That's exactly what was to happen to Dardo.

I went to pick up the test results, to a very old section of the hospital where the labs are, in the middle of a large, abandoned garden. The hospital was built in 1867. There's a new wing, all steel and glass, with automatic doors and large, shiny mosaics, but the old wing is still kept up and used, dutifully refurbished and modernized with the latest technology. Nevertheless, as I walked along paths invaded by weeds and cats, among faded, red gabled roofs and narrow windows, I wouldn't have been surprised to see Louis Pasteur and Marie Curie in white smocks, with the broad foreheads and stern, dignified faces of the scientists of their times. I waited at a window to pick up the envelope with the diagnosis.

Sebastián, a twenty-one-year-old medical student and Dardo's son from his first marriage, came along with me. Quality of life, the oncologist had said from across the desk, which he couldn't quite reach because of his corpulence. Above all, pain control: they would try different painkillers until they found the most effective one. When we left, Sebastián's expression was stony. He refused to go with me to a bar and discuss it over a drink. He had to get to class.

There was enough money to deal with things. Dardo continued to collect his salary from the firm; I controlled my emotions with pills, and a period of calm and improvement of symptoms ensued, a respite from the illness. The pain had practically disappeared. One morning, after discharging him from the hospital, they operated on the broken bone in his arm and managed to connect both sections with a pin. Dardo began using his right hand again; he could write, although his handwriting was somewhat shaky, and he could use a knife and fork. He read tirelessly, took long naps. I realized that this respite is called the plateau of an illness: the days go by calmly, routinely. I remember the silence that reigned in the house during the early afternoon of those days, while Dardo napped. I paced up and down the living room, straightening things, arranging books on shelves. At that hour a triangular sunbeam fell on the table, shining on a fruit bowl filled with green apples.

I don't remember when the symptoms began. Another search for painkillers, more aggressive ones this time, with more dangerous side effects. Dardo could still walk with a cane; soon there would be a wheelchair. I took care of him, bathed him, put him to bed between fragrant sheets, prepared exquisite, delicate meals for him. I gave up all activities that obliged me to leave the house. I rigged up a study for myself ("study" sounds too pompous; let's just say a workspace) in an odd room that one reached by crossing the kitchen and a little patio. I've always lived in rented houses that I can never discover entirely, and that doesn't bother me too much because I know that at any given moment, I'll abandon them for others, but, to compensate, I appropriate those things I can't take with me when I move, storing them in my heart. A built-in piece of furniture, a balcony. It's likely that in the place where this flimsy room was (one of the walls was made of particle board, painted to simulate whitewash), there was once just a wide balcony, and they built the room for storage.

Happiness is a strange thing. Even during Dardo's illness, I was happy in that room. It was an absolutely humble room: I tacked posters and photographs to the walls, gathered some old furniture together and a radio that was just as old but had very good sound. There was a single little window, like a cell window, way up high, through which you could detect the color of the sky. I've always liked gray skies, more than ever in those days: they matched my melancholy and promised the delights of a rain that would beat against the windowpane. If I opened the door to the little patio, I could get good ventilation because it was on the seventh floor, and there were no other tall buildings around. There was a mattress for my yoga practice, a chaise longue for stretching out to read on warm days, drowse and later return to my poor old typewriter to write. My days began at five a.m.; at that hour I awoke spontaneously, had coffee, and started working in the little room while Dardo slept.

They gave him one year to live. It turned out to be exactly eleven and a half months. So, the remainder of that winter went by, then an entire spring, a whole summer, and, in the middle of the following winter, Dardo, who until then had always been there, who had been with me for over twenty years, was no longer there, ever again.

When my tears come flooding, I know I'm crying not just about Dardo's death but also for his pain, my pain, and the memory, now enclosed in a bubble, of our life together, with its happiness and unhappiness. For example, that Sunday, many years before, when the children still lived with us and brought their friends over; the house was transformed into a summer camp: there were makeshift beds all over with mattresses on the floor, a mess in the kitchen, and a swarm of people of various ages who expected different things of me, but mostly food. I simply escaped for a few hours, sitting at the Molino Café. I had brought along a notebook and a pen. Useless. I stayed there for a long time, staring at some paintings on the walls by unknown painters and the marble staircase that led to the banquet room, remembering the days when I used to travel deliberately to that corner of Rivadavia and Callao to have tea with sandwiches and cookies at five in the afternoon. I've never been able to work in noisy places; I can't shut myself off, like other people who choose to do their reading or writing in bars. I'm too interested in the people sitting at the other tables, especially if I notice that they're arguing. I invent scenarios, take sides – how could I possibly write, too! By the time I returned home, the visitors had left.

One day, after a doctor's appointment, Dardo got up the nerve to look at himself in the elevator mirror. I hadn't realized that since the onset, or rather the diagnosis, of his illness, he'd never again looked at his reflection in a mirror; at one point we wanted to shave off his beard, so we had a barber come to the house, and from then on his son Sebastián or some other young male family member would shave him. When he saw himself in the elevator mirror, he was shocked by his thin, gray face, his twisted, bent body. But Dardo had always been slight, thin, and had a noticeable curvature of the spine. Sometime we would sit and look at old photos that revealed bits of our lives before we met. I remember one where he looked skinny and pale, dressed in shorts and sandals, standing in the sunlight on a hilltop, with a slight smile just for the picture.

I no longer heard him walking around the house, and that was the part of his absence that affected me most. Even after we moved, I was still surprised not to hear his footsteps anymore, not to see him appear in the living room doorway. At night, after taking off his white shirt and dark tie and putting on a caramel-colored sweater, very comfy and soft to the touch, and his threadbare corduroy pants, Dardo would sit down on a sofa we had, and which no longer exists, a burgundy-colored, velveteen sofa with a faint odor of cat piss that we tried to get rid of for years, in vain. He would read or watch television. We'd bought the sofa in a secondhand furniture store in Floresta. When we sat down to try it, we hadn't noticed the smell. We liked its deep burgundy color, those nice, soft pillows, and we imagined it with ivory-toned, crocheted antimacassars, which we never managed to get, on the armrests.

Today, for the first time in so many years, in my hotel room at the spa, I once again heard the infinite sweetness of *Trois Leçons de Ténèbres*. I hadn't heard it since the days when it accompanied me in my workroom during Dardo's illness. I used to work at the other end of the house, and we had an intercom system like the ones they use to monitor a sleeping baby in another part of the house. By this time Dardo was a complete invalid. He showed no external signs of the illness – no swelling, no odor – just tremendous weight loss and paleness. Only the doctors could see on the X-rays how the cancer had done its work on his bones. Our clinician, who never smoked when he attended his patients, asked my permission to smoke a cigarette the first time he saw one of Dardo's X-rays.

I started working in my room off the terrace before six a.m., and Dardo would call me on the little intercom device around nine. I would dash to our bedroom, and there, sprawling, rather than sitting up between the sheets, would be Dardo, who greeted me, incredibly, with a big smile.

Three times a week the ambulance from Social Services came to take him to the hospital for chemotherapy. I went with him. Two powerful men positioned him on the stretcher and covered him with a light-blue sheet. We took the elevator downstairs, and some neighbor or other would always come over to ask him how he was doing. I wished they hadn't; they stared at him from their comfortable vertical position, pausing in their agile stride toward the street to take notice of that emaciated, prostrate man, motionless on the stretcher but invariably polite, attempting to reply. I became practical during this ordeal: on arriving at the hospital, while the orderlies carried Dardo to his cubicle in the chemotherapy section, I filled out forms along with other individuals who were also relatives of the sick, sick themselves with suffering and exhaustion. It was still easy for the nurse to locate a vein to hold the needle through which the medication would drip. Later it became increasingly difficult. Dardo always fell asleep, and he slept for quite a while, during which time I would read or have coffee in the cafeteria. Two or three hours later we would return home. He smiled, as I, in the folding seat next to the stretcher in the ambulance, took inventory of the different parts of my being. Mind: clear, alert, uncluttered. Body: suffused with the pleasure of getting away from the hospital, the pleasure produced by tranquilizers and the knowledge that Dardo wasn't suffering. Conscience: at peace.

Dardo was happy whenever we returned home after chemotherapy, on the ambulance stretcher, covered with a light-blue sheet, joking with the orderlies. Yes, happy, because the chemo didn't cause him any discomfort and happy at the prospect of going back to his cozy house and playing Chinese checkers with me. Dardo always won, just as he always beat me at chess, but I insisted that we play because I really didn't care about winning. I've never cared much about winning or losing at games, and that annoys some people. They can't forgive me for playing for the sheer fun of it and for letting my thoughts stray to anything else. They don't like to play with someone who couldn't care less about winning or losing. Later on, in my workroom, those voices repeated the lessons of darkness. A few months after that, I would find myself crying before the freshly turned dirt of the grave and the bronze plaque that simply said *Dardo*.

Dardo before his illness, when he walked around the house and appeared in the dining room every morning with his impeccable shirt, his already thinned hair, dampened and carefully combed, the newspaper open to the Entertainment section. I gladly let him choose the films, the concerts, the guests. Those were the days, long before the diagnosis, when we would be awakened by the light filtering through the blinds into our room. I remember lying on my side, very close to Dardo, awakening and looking at that gentle sunbeam on my hip. One more minute of contact between our bodies. I allowed myself a little more sleep while Dardo showered, and later, when I emerged from the bathroom, I found him standing before the open closet door, choosing a tie.

Cecilia.

Your footsteps, Dardo.

Cecilia.

Yes, Dardo, I hear you. Your footsteps approaching from our bedroom. The caramel-colored sweater, its soft wool against my cheek when I rest my head against your shoulder, the two of us sitting on the burgundy velvet sofa that miraculously doesn't smell of cat piss.

We have to take the kids to a birthday party and pick them up afterward.

Cecilia.

Yes, Dardo, I hear you.

I'll go pick up Tomás; I have to leave at eight.

The warm air of the last bit of afternoon sun, and the oven just lit, the smell of apple flan coming from the kitchen. Yes, Dardo, I hear you.

Will you go pick him up?

Yes, Dardo, and you can pick up Francisco, yes, I'm making apple flan, it's autumn, it's starting to grow a bit cold, I hear you, Dardo, I hear your footsteps. What time did Sebastián say he's coming home? What's that business about your having to die, Dardo? Did anyone tell me I'd be standing in the street, hiding from the neighbors, a few steps away from the entrance to the building, in order to avoid seeing you cross the threshold in a coffin?

Cecilia.

Yes, Dardo.

It's raining in Buenos Aires. Steve had to go on a trip, and I decided to spend the weekend here. I explained to the spa directors that I needed to go, and they agreed immediately.

I feel a bit lonely in my apartment in Palermo, but I enjoy small pleasures: making myself a cup of tea or preparing a sandwich in my own kitchen. Here I don't have to practice the permanent "contact with nature" that I can't escape at the spa; here I can go to the movies and have coffee with a friend (espresso with cream, for me), and we can tell each other our life stories, not mine or hers, but just stories about life, our own philosophies, filled with originality and clichés, because that's why one sits down and has a cup of coffee with a friend. It's noisy inside the café, and noise filters in from the street; people are shouting at each other in order to be heard; the waitress brings some tiny cookies along with the demitasses. On the way home I run some errands in the neighborhood, trying to remember everything I need so that I won't have to go back downstairs again, as if it were a question of descending from a mountain rather than from the fifth floor. I go to the supermarket, where for a while I feel happy and protected (who knows why?). The same thing happens to me in supermarkets all over the world. I feel like I could buy everything they have on display in such pretty containers, which is a lie, of course, but I always buy something extra: that jar of aged mustard with green pepper, that whipped, nonfat yogurt with mixed berries that later on I decide I don't like as I watch it disappear down the drain in a stream of water. Then to the post office: you have to take a number. I get 67, and they're only up to 24, so I go out to the street and look into the window of a dress shop where they sell ladies' clothing, all gray, brown, and black. There's also a deep-purple sweater. Black and purple used to be for mourning and semi-mourning – who'd ever think of wearing them unless someone had died? And then to the fascist's photocopy shop on Güemes Street because I want to take along a story to read at the spa, and it's in a book that weighs a ton. As he makes the copy, the owner explains that there's no reason to criticize our government officials because people need them, and that one should differentiate between those people who've been in this country for five hundred years, like him (what he's doing in this photocopy dump, I couldn't say), and those who came from "outside" and don't know anything about how the fatherland was created. Finally, to the little bakery next to my house, where they sell croissants, the kind you can find only in Buenos Aires. I go upstairs and settle in at the keyboard again, and from there I can see plenty of sky through the window.

I miss Steve; I miss him even though that makes me feel a little bit afraid. And what if suddenly I feel as though I can't live without him? And what then if I lose him? I resolve everything by getting up to go to the kitchen and make coffee, even before starting work. The telephone rings. It's Steve, telling me enthusiastically that he'll be back at the spa tomorrow and hopes to meet me there. That wasn't my plan, but his full, pleasant voice makes me tremble from head to toe. When, when, when, will I learn to protect myself?

The doctor wanted Dardo to die at home, under my care, with only the technical assistance of tranquilizers and an oxygen tank that he emptied in very little time and which had to be exchanged for another. In order to ensure that Social Services authorized the oxygen, I took the subway to their offices on Luis Sáenz Peña Boulevard. I walked down Florida and Perú without anyone's being able to guess that I was carrying death on my shoulders.

"Can't you send the tank today?"

"Today's Saturday, *señora*. There aren't many ambulances available."

"Today's Saturday? But he can't breathe!"

"Monday morning."

"He has to breathe today! Saturday! And Sunday, too!"

I cried and shouted at the window. The offices are below street level. By the time I went upstairs to the second floor with the authorization I needed, I had regained my composure. I went out to the street and began walking swiftly toward the subway station. The two poor guys who brought a tank over every day brought the last one upstairs the same night Dardo died, walking up seven flights because the elevators were broken. I gave the sweaty men some water and double the usual tip.

It was then that Dardo said, "I'm tired."

Anyone who has ever attended the dying knows that those two words, *I'm tired*, are an announcement of the end.

The doctor came for the last time, although he didn't know it; he had no way of guessing that it was the last time we would sit down at the dining room table with its bowl of green apples in the middle to talk about Dardo.

"He should be dead by now," the doctor said. "But he hasn't died because he doesn't talk about it. As soon as he talks about it, he'll disappear like a sigh."

It made no difference that Dardo didn't talk. He never spoke about his death, but he died anyway.

The doctor was a very busy man, but that day he didn't seem to be in a hurry. At last he stood up; maybe he added some other remark; maybe I cried. Finally, he said, "I'll never forget you, Cecilia." He liked me because I had agreed to take care of Dardo during the last weeks of his life, at home and in his own bed, in our bed, where he would die in a natural way. One of those nights I awoke at four in the morning, and I knew Dardo was dead, without even turning on the light. Perhaps because the tenuous murmur of his breath in the air was missing. I would like to remember where the oxygen mask was on the bed. Could it have fallen? Did Dardo have enough strength to have pulled it off himself? Dardo went away with his voice, his footsteps, his caramel-colored sweater, his oxygen mask.

Sebastián went with me to see him. Dardo was still lying in bed. He was wearing his watch. It was an old watch he had bought many years before in Rome, at the flea market in Porta Portese, from some Russian exiles who sold chess sets, coral necklaces, and those dolls that fit inside one another. We had bought two identical watches, and we wore them like twins whose mama dresses them alike. They were big, windup watches, with Arabic numerals (we never liked Roman numerals), and the numerals were big, also, so that we could read them without glasses. Sebastián and I looked at each other and decided that Dardo shouldn't wear that watch in the grave. I gave it to Sebastián, he put it on at that very moment, and we embraced, crying. The watch had accompanied Dardo to the other world, and now it had returned.

I've just finished making myself some broth with rice that's turned out tasting like the ones they gave Dardo at the hospital. Watery, no salt.

"Eat the soup, Dardo."

"I don't feel like it, Cecilia."

"But it'll make you feel better, and then you'll sleep for a while."

The day that Social Services sent the hospital bed the doctor had prescribed, Dardo cried like a little boy. He knew. He never spoke of his death, but he knew. Then he fell asleep. Silent and pale, we looked at that enormous, hulking thing. By nightfall the hospital bed was no longer there because we sent it back. It was tall and bulky, with lots of levers. Dardo would have lain there, exposed as on an operating table, terribly alone. He continued to sleep on his side of our bed, which was the right side if you looked at it from the doorway. And I slept next to him, night after night, with the help of my pills, until that early morning when I awoke knowing he was dead. Never, after we shared our bed again, did I dare touch him. I just kissed him on the forehead, on the cheek.

Every time I open the top drawer of my desk, I see a picture of Dardo and me, on vacation in Brazil, with our happy, tanned faces. He has his hand on my shoulder; we had almost certainly already drunk our first caipirinha of the day. Dardo didn't want us to take that vacation; he thought we couldn't afford it, and he was probably right. But he was as careless as I was with money and equally incapable of making big plans for the future. For two weeks we went around barefoot and in bathing suits, on a little private beach near Florianópolis. The horizon of the bay was nearly always blurred by a light gray haze.

The sea. It was my mother who taught me to love it. Whenever we walked back to our hotel on vacation, she would suddenly say to me, "Look at the color of the sea," and, what a miracle, it was no longer cold blue like early that same morning when we arrived at the beach but, rather, a marvelous steely shade. Dardo had a mother, too.

"Me, let me do it," Berta would say about any domestic chore whenever she came to visit us. "I have nothing to do." And that old, skinny woman with fabulous blue eyes that she emphasized simply by putting on lipstick, like those who are truly beautiful, that lady who never had anything to do and therefore was always doing something, made tea and toast and later washed the dishes.

There we were, Berta and I, in the living room, in the late afternoon light, having tea and toast. It made me happy to share that Sunday afternoon moment with her, as Dardo took his interminable siesta. He must have been sick already without our knowing; if not, why did he need to sleep so much? Had I taken good care of him? Didn't the doctor once ask us why we hadn't tried transaminase? Hadn't the doctor once ordered a test that was never done? And if it had been done, would they have discovered that tumor before it metastasized? If I had paid more attention to what the doctor told Dardo, could Dardo have been saved?

When Dardo died and my older children returned from Europe, I began to notice, with a terrible mixture of fear and weakness, Federico's violent eruptions. At the time Federico was seventeen and suffering, according to the doctors, from "pathological pain." I never really understood what *pathological* meant, but that label was enough to explain some of his strange, brutal reactions. He seemed more furious than sad; his schoolwork was a disaster, and he would disappear for hours at a time or else fill the house with friends, playing deafening music. Federico, don't play that music, I wanted to tell him – your father has just died. But my strength had left me, and I also blamed myself for not having paid enough attention to him while I was taking care of Dardo during the nightmare of his illness. The specialists I consulted told me that the loss of a father was a terrible thing at age seventeen. But what could be done? Set limits and give him plenty of love, they replied. I didn't know at the time how incredibly often I would hear about that combination of love and limits. I felt dry, empty, and weak; I could hardly display much love even if I felt it, much less set limits.

Dardo's mother, Berta, and I established a routine once more, but it wasn't the same routine of tea and toast at home on Sundays. Now I was the one who went over to her house with my old, portable Olivetti typewriter, to keep her company and to try to continue working far away from Federico's full-blast music and his foul moods. I couldn't impose silence in my own house, which was gradually being invaded by a group of adolescents who felt authorized, because of my own lack of control over the situation, to stay till all hours, eating, drinking beer, making a mess and ruining things, without ever thinking of washing their dirty glasses and dishes, without thinking that it was a weekday, that they should have been studying or in any case showing some respect for the mourning period in the house of a friend who had just lost his father. Their world was different, and I watched them with my arms folded, unable to react except for the occasional extemporaneous outburst, for which Federico would harshly reproach me afterward.

Berta enjoyed it when I visited her in her apartment on Bulnes Street, an old, dark, disorderly apartment with drawers full of photographs and medicines; after her terrible loss, she had no energy to go anywhere. When I returned home in mid-afternoon, I often found my living room in darkness, with the blinds closed, boys and girls dancing amid alcohol fumes and cigarette smoke, along with some other odor I couldn't identify. Exhausted, defeated, I locked myself in my room.

As soon as I heard the taxi's horn, I put on a raincoat and went downstairs to the street. Steve had decided to come to Buenos Aires to pick me up, and I ran to greet him at the airport. The cool wind and the rain whipped my face and blew away my ghosts in a single gust.

The driver opened the car door for me, and during the entire trip I didn't stop chatting with him for one moment; we talked about the weather, the traffic that gets worse whenever it rains, and a son of his who was studying architecture. Once we passed the housing projects and reached the green area, carefully tended and planted with trees like a garden leading to the airport, I felt my blood flowing through my veins again. The plane would arrive in a half-hour; I went up to the cafeteria, deciding it was an excellent occasion for a cup of coffee and some toast. A grilled ham and cheese sandwich, Argentine style. That would be the first thing I'd make Steve taste. We'd get to the *empanadas* and *locro* soon enough, but it would be better to begin with something blander, something, in any case, that could be found only in Buenos Aires. A woman pushing her cart full of luggage had to ask us politely to let her go by when I saw Steve at last and we embraced, oblivious to the world and blocking the path to the exit.

A gringo is always a gringo. When Steve found out how far it was from the airport to my house in Palermo, he decided to store his luggage in a locker until later and set off to see the city right then and there. He had a map of Argentina and a city map of the Federal District in his pocket, and he had already planned the program for the day: Recoleta and Palermo in the morning; after lunch and a rest at my place, San Telmo. Dinner in La Boca. I could have objected to the plan because it was raining like crazy and because I had fantasized about being alone with him, but at that moment, if he'd asked me to go to Puerto Madryn and return the same day, I would have done it with the same smile; I couldn't take my eyes off him. There he was, without a trace of fatigue on his happy, tanned face.

And so, standing in the rain, our wet hands clasped, we stared at the Church of El Pilar. Later, as I watched him sleeping beside me, I thought that sometimes happiness is simple and understandable.

When we got up to go to dinner, Steve had given up on the idea of going to La Boca; we picked a nice little place close to home. But we followed the next day's itinerary, and the one after that, to the letter.

Steve admired, enjoyed, never got bored, depressed, or anguished, as I sometimes do when I travel. One night I cooked dinner. I made my famous stuffed *colita de cuadril*, a cut of meat that needs to be roasted quickly, on a high flame, stuffed with a mixture of bread soaked in milk, eggs, garlic, and parsley. I assured him it was a typical Argentine dish, and I actually think it is; I've never found anything like it anywhere else. I served it with buttered potatoes boiled in their skin, and I gave it an Italian touch with a salad of shredded carrots and finely chopped fennel. For dessert, Passover blintzes, which is the only Jewish dish I know how to make. They're pancakes filled with sweetened cheese and raisins, covered with confectioner's sugar and cinnamon. Bah, how should I know if they're authentic blintzes, but someone said, and they were right, that it doesn't pay to worry about authenticity. The best part was that, while I prepared them, a pair of strong arms embraced me unexpectedly from behind. With my floury hands and my cooking apron, I took the sip Steve offered me from his own glass, and suddenly I was afraid of so much domestic complacency. What if we could never be apart again and life brought us more suffering? It was a short-lived fear: it disappeared with the next little sip.

Steve felt very comfortable in Buenos Aires. He wasn't one of those unmistakable Nordic tourists you see wandering along Calle Florida in shorts and sunglasses with a liter of milk in one hand in the middle of August because it's the middle of summer in their own country. On the other hand, he does certain North American things that I like: if we eat at home, he never waits for me to take his dirty plate and silverware into the kitchen; he throws out the leftover food, rinses the plate under a stream of warm water (he can't understand why I don't have a dishwasher), and, finally, uncertain, leaves everything in the sink. Those determined feminists have achieved something in the last hundred years!

Sometimes I wonder if we're a couple. We sleep together, we spend plenty of time together, we talk a lot – finally, after a lifetime of not being able to find a man who was willing to dance to old songs . . . These thoughts never bother me too much. We'll return to the spa in a few days, and neither of us would think of doing otherwise, not because we're expecting a cure but because the wounds we suffered were open for a long time.

While Steve goes to the beach, I walk toward my waterfall and fall asleep or simply doze beside the stream before starting homeward. Memories of Dardo always return, and I don't do anything to avoid them.

To whom did he speak in his delirium, during his last few days of life? Perhaps to his dead father, that serious, sad, and intelligent man whom I never met. Dardo told me so many times how he would watch him take off his shoes at night, sitting on the edge of the bed and saying, "Ugh, what a day!" Dardo's father always found his days very long. His mother, on the other hand, didn't complain; she always chose to remain at home, cleaning and cooking, and his father went out alone, well dressed. How strange, it never occurred to Dardo that perhaps his father went out to meet other women, that he might have had a lover or visited a prostitute or spoken to some woman he'd met over a casual remark about the cover of whatever magazine both of them were browsing through at a kiosk, the beginning of a conversation that would be continued in the "family" section of a bar. Maybe he'd even taken that woman, as lonely as he himself was, to a room in a by-the-hour hotel. No, Dardo wanted to believe his father strolled along Calle Florida in his impeccable silk shirt and custom-made suit (the shirts were custom-made, too) just so he could see his image reflected in the shop windows.

Berta was quite old when she died, and life can't be prolonged eternally. But her son's death took away what seemed to be her only reason for existing. She'd never again chop veal liver into tiny pieces, later adding diced onion, salt, and oil, or contemplate Dardo with devotion from across the table as he silently devoured it. If what existed between them wasn't a romance, then nothing is. On Saturdays and Sundays Berta occupied her place in our home with great dignity, with the limitless dignity of the humble.

Sitting next to the stream by the waterfall in the rainforest, I recalled the banks of a different river, in the Paraná Delta. Out there you never know what the river might bring: a floating tangle of grass, an old shoe, a little wave with dirty foam, a supply boat with its dark-skinned, thin, silent owner propelling his old launch along with a single oar and doing me a big favor by selling me some lettuce, a package of *yerba mate*. Dardo and I had fallen asleep on a thin mattress; in the middle of the night we heard distant thunder and rain falling gently on the leaves. We awoke with the light filtering through the old curtains and went outside to get the coffee and the bathing suit that had been left out in the weather all night. We adored those precarious weekends, in full possession and enactment of our love.

Last night I dreamed of Dardo. In my dream he was alive, but he wasn't the Dardo I knew: agile, clever. No, not at all! And he and I weren't in the simple orderliness of our house, cups on saucers, bread in the breadbox, after a good night's sleep following some conjugal delight, as calm and pleasant as waves on a tranquil sea.

No. In the dream we were in a room that looked more like the rooms of that dreary house where one morning I received the news that my father had died. In a room like that, without windows, with a door leading who knows where; in a dream, a door can lead to a patio or to a hospital corridor with an obese nurse, as serious as a judge, waddling along with a little pail of instruments in her hand. The door can just as easily lead to a void. And there we were, Dardo and I, happy to be together after so many years without touching one another.

In the dream Dardo was alive. Dardo *was*. And the room was mostly white. The walls were white and bare; there were white sheets on the bed, and we were dressed in old-fashioned, coarse, white flannel nightclothes, the kind they sold in little shops in Buenos Aires fifty years ago, like the deformed nightgowns of my school days, which I would leave under my pillow when I made my bed and got dressed, before going out to the chilly freedom of the street. In the dream Dardo and I looked at each other without speaking.

Our grandmas used to loosen their corsets and place a crown of raw potato slices tied up with a handkerchief on their foreheads in order to get rid of headaches, and they didn't say, "It changed my life!" because no one said those things, but the first two or three times the remedy worked. Later it lost its effectiveness. Then they would try vinegar rubs on their foreheads. And later chloroform, and eventually suicide. Now there are classes, workshops, alternative medicine, horoscopes, astrological cards, spas, with their promise of curing illnesses, the tedium of existence, and death.

I've been at the spa for two months now. Lately I've begun to feel, with great disillusionment, a recurrence of some of my symptoms. Suddenly I lose interest in everything; I stop enjoying the rain-forest and the sea; I don't feel like reading. They warned me this would happen, but, like anyone who starts a treatment, I thought it was magical; I almost felt like shouting, "It changed my life!" The fact is, my stomach hurts again when I get up, my nose is running, and I'm dying of weariness as soon as dinner's over, and the next morning it takes a real effort to get ready for my walk in the rain-forest. It's true that all this happens only on those days when Steve returns to Los Angeles on business.

Steve and I never talk about our belated romance as a salvation. We simply enjoy it like a gift we give each other, without asking for or expecting anything else. Each one has to manage for himself... Bah, ideas I learned from the children's magazine *Billiken* when I was a kid. At the bottom of every page, beneath an instructive story or a little anecdote, you could read: "God helps those who help themselves." "The Devil finds work for idle hands." "The force of will is the backbone of man's destiny." At the bottom of the next page it simply stated the height of Mount Aconcagua, but that didn't seem strange to me: what mattered was to acquire knowledge.

It's no use trying to forget, the spa director told me. I knew it, but during my first weeks at this place I had forgotten my most recent problems, the ones that brought me here, submerging myself in the sweet melancholy of my memories of Dardo. We felt so good, my body and me! It makes sense that they don't promise anyone a total cure – just as no one could expect Federico to be completely cured. In order to cure him, they say, you'd have to modify his DNA and change his childhood, and that, as far as I know, is impossible. But in more serious cases than ours there could be a solution: they wanted to try an unusual cure on Steve's son: they wanted to change his memories. I don't know what method they used, but the idea frightened me. Donald's mother and Steve didn't agree to it. What would they make him "remember"? That his real parents were other people who had died in an accident? That he had spent a happy childhood somewhere else? And what about me? What would I like to remember if I could change my memories? When I really think about it, I'd rather remember my sad childhood as long as I'd remain the same, just as, although you may complain about the mother you were stuck with, you wouldn't want to be any other woman's child because that would make you a different person. Maybe that's what therapy's all about, becoming a different person. I glanced into the tiny mirror I carried in my purse.

Steve, like a fairy godmother, had them bring a computer, my most beloved books, and my most familiar music to my room at the little hotel, but at the spa I still miss Buenos Aires's stale air. I miss everything my eyes see when I'm there, and I pause in my work for a moment to think about my study in the apartment where I live now, on a peaceful street in the Palermo district, so different from the study I had in the house where Dardo died, where I listened to the *Lessons of Darkness* and watched the sky through a tiny window. Nevertheless, the room I use as my study always resembles the ones I had in my previous houses: the same disorderly shelves full of books, bills to pay, in plain sight so that I won't forget. The only things that change through the years and the many moves are the ones I hang on the walls. When I take my eyes from the screen, I see an old Italian poster on the wall that says *Femminismo*, with a 1900-vintage woman pulling a pair of men's trousers over her long, lacy underpants, and a cardboard Pierrot with movable arms and legs joined to its body with thumbtacks. The Pierrot hangs from a string, and sometimes the breeze or the fan turns it around, and it's nothing more than a brown cardboard cutout – then I hurriedly turn it back again. On the opposite wall is a large, framed poster, a reproduction of a painting that was hidden in Germany for many years during the time of the Nazis, together with other works by Jewish painters. It's a picture of an old watchmaker at his worktable. The man has laid aside his delicate instruments and his dismantled watches in order to read the newspaper. I don't know what the large headlines say in Yiddish, but since the painting is dated 1914, one can imagine the reason for the stupefaction and anguish on the old man's fine face. I don't look at him as I work, but I feel him taking care of me, as though he were the ghost of a grandfather or great-grandfather guarding my back. The suffragette and the Pierrot, despite their fragility, also protect me from falling into the void.

I've moved so many times, I can't remember how many, and I can't get used to it. Even if it's to go to a better place, moving always exhausts me. I get lost among so many old things that we stored for so long and that suddenly come to light, like sick, old people who only go out on Sunday and remain hidden for the rest of the week. I look at those typical, ugly boxes the moving company provides as I carry them out to the street. Then, just like when I'm about to take a trip, I'm neither here nor there; I'm in the street, and the worst part of it is I feel like that's really my place. "That woman hasn't got a roof over her head," the landlords might say; "She's a chronic tenant." Even the word *tenant* sounds weak to me, inconsistent.

In this second jaunt to Buenos Aires Steve devotes himself to his hobby: he photographs and videotapes the city. And my book progresses because I can spend whole days at the computer.

When Tomás and Francisco went back to Europe, leaving me truly alone with Dardo (Sebastián was about to graduate from medical school, and Federico, practically expelled from school, spent his days who knows where, hardly ever seeing his father), I decided to consult a new psychiatrist.

"I'm not going to be able to deal with it," I told her.

"Of course you'll be able to," she replied. "Besides, how can you be sure your husband will die before you do?"

She was right. According to the doctor's prognosis, he still had a few months left, but meanwhile I could have an accident or be struck by an aneurysm. Who could be sure one of those things wouldn't happen? That psychiatrist knew how to put a stop to my anxiety. I left her office feeling like a chip tossed onto the roulette wheel of life and death until the croupier says that's it. Either before or after Dardo, I, too, would die, and everything would continue in its proper place – for example, that oversized book with its white cover and black letters, two plays by Sartre in an old Losada edition, that I see on the shelf every time I interrupt this work to think. When Tomás and Federico were kids and I took them to the park or to the beach, that book went with me on more than one occasion, like so many other beloved books I like to take along when I travel. They always intrigue me, but I never manage to read more than a little bit, and on my next trip I have to start from the beginning so that I don't get the characters mixed up. When I used to go out with the children, I had to be careful not to let them out of my sight, not to let them get too close to the swings and be clobbered, and not to throw away the vegetable croquettes I used to take along so that they wouldn't fill up on hot dogs or hamburgers, which meant I could never advance in my reading. But those books are witnesses to different moments in my life, bits of myself.

Against the icy wind
the poor woman,
that beast of burden,
searches for dry firewood
to warm the good man.

The good man who will die
a natural death.

Dardo wouldn't die a natural death, after all, but he would die in a natural way. After that month in the hospital, we took him home to die. In a very natural way, after eleven months of that strange life in which I devoted myself to caring for him, early one morning I found him, as usual, lying by my side, with the candid expression of a child, his eyes closed, and that half-smile of those who are sleeping peacefully, only this time forever.

It's typical for the living to speak of the dead. Who will speak of me when they find my lifeless body? And later, when the pain of death becomes the deeper pain of absence, who will miss my voice, my footsteps?

When Dardo died, only Federico and I were left in the house. Our first move after Dardo's death: we found a smaller apartment, freshly painted, and with an oven that didn't burn my forearms. In Buenos Aires average apartments (not necessarily the poorest ones and certainly not the most luxurious, the kind that are advertised as "Ideal for Diplomat" in the classifieds) are always nearly identical. They all have that famous living-dining room combination, one or more bedrooms off a hallway, a slightly more than modest kitchen, and a single bathroom where the faucet leaks for more or less time, depending on the negligence of the occupants.

In the apartment where I went to live with Federico, I couldn't fall asleep until after midnight because of the noise he and his friends made. One night, at one a.m., after having heard a loud, disturbing noise, I got up to discover several girls in the bathroom, making themselves up to go out. As there was just one mirror above the sink and they wanted to see their full-length reflections, one had climbed up onto the sink and yanked the mirror from the wall. It dangled there, the debris from the destruction all over the floor. The one responsible for the accident was sitting on the closed toilet seat, overcome with laughter. I wanted to scream, but I couldn't emit a single sound: in a tiny voice I managed to say, you'll fix this tomorrow. Of course, I was the one who paid for the repair.

Federico, who was old enough to be a senior but who was repeating his sophomore year after having repeated his freshman year as well, and who therefore had already spent four years in high school, was always on the verge of being expelled for truancy. I had been struggling with his behavior problems, which for years were attributed to adolescence, that time of life when young people are afflicted with a kind of physiological insanity, leaving their parents perplexed and unable to find explanations or useful advice in child-rearing texts. Every so often I'd have to go see the principal, a kindly, considerate woman, and beg her not to throw Federico out.

"But he's already got fifty-eight absences," the woman said patiently (I think the maximum allowable was forty-five).

"Yes, but my husband's illness was terrible, and losing a father at seventeen . . . ," I recited, "and his older brothers aren't here, and I'm alone with him . . ."

"There's only one reason we haven't thrown him out yet, *señora*. It's our job to keep kids off the streets."

"Why don't you talk to him?"

"I have, *señora*. But you're the one who has to set limits. Let him know that you love him but that he can't do anything he wants to."

The important thing was that they didn't expel him. My soul returned to my body.

But that good woman didn't know the extent of Federico's conduct or my inadequate response to that conduct. I don't think I understood what *symbiosis* means. I pretended not to know that Federico was stealing from me; I restricted myself to hiding the money carefully, although I always left some on hand so that he could take it; I bought him his heavy metal or country or punk clothing in stores where they sold those fleeting fashions at unheard-of prices. I discovered that Federico was paying his bar bills and those of his friends – copious beers and sandwiches – with my money.

I felt as disoriented as the time when, three years earlier, Federico joined a sort of neighborhood gang led by two older girls, heavyset, nasty-looking young women who gathered lots of kids like him in their houses. The other kids' mothers talked to me, expressing their fears. They were neighborhood women, simple, unsophisticated; one of them confided that she was worried because her son was so small (he was, in fact, thirteen but looked no more than ten), and she feared premature sexual relations could stunt his genitalia.

As the dinner hour approached, I left work to look for Federico and drag him home. I found him on a corner, leaning against a car. He glared at me silently, haughtily, his hands in his pockets. I started to say something; he turned his face aside, not responding. Finally, still looking the other way, he deigned to come back home. One day I spoke to the girls, telling them I forbade Federico to keep on wasting entire afternoons with them and the others. They were two slovenly-looking fat girls with greasy hair and swollen eyes, dressed in stained sweatsuits and shabby sneakers with untied shoelaces. It wasn't that sort of deliberate negligence some adolescents affect (those exorbitant, torn, holey jeans you see in shop windows): the girls' carelessness was far from whimsical; it was pure sloppiness and filth.

"Okay," one of them replied to my protests. "I don't want no problems. If you won't let him, he won't come to my house no more."

She went into the house, slamming the door behind her.

Yes, of course they were initiating the boys sexually. In a movie this fact would have seemed perfectly natural to me and might have even amused me, but in Federico's case it was combined with a new sort of rude, rebellious behavior toward Dardo and me that we didn't know how to handle. Now I wouldn't be surprised to learn that they were also initiating the boys in drugs and alcohol, although at the time it never crossed my mind.

Dardo and I were experienced, since we had both been parents before, but my older boys' rebellion and that of Dardo's son could always be resolved with a few raised voices and the well-timed slap. When I joined my life with Dardo's, Tomás and Francisco had two fathers: Daniel, my ex, and Dardo, who loved them very much and spent long hours talking to them. We saw Sebastián, Dardo's son, who was younger than my older two and only five years older than Federico, on weekends. He was a studious, diligent boy who, as far as I could tell, went through the vicissitudes of youth with moderation, although as soon as he became independent enough to do so, he adopted the habit of disappearing for long periods of time. Federico was different: nothing seemed to go right with him.

When the neighborhood gang was formed, he was fourteen. Seventeen when Dardo died and we moved away. I placed great hope in the change of location; I thought it would be good for us to get away from the place where we had all suffered so greatly. For a few weeks we enjoyed furnishing and decorating the new apartment. Sometimes Federico would accompany me, and I would have to put the brakes on what he asked me to buy, suggestions that went far beyond my ascetic lifestyle: he wanted a little bar, a curved sofa for one corner of the living room. They were very expensive furnishings, garish and pretentious, and I refused. I could still calmly say no to my son's whims, despite the grim atmosphere my refusals created.

One frigid night I left the house, all bundled up and elegant, with a book in my purse. I've never enjoyed going out alone, but I had been told what I needed to do to overcome my anguish and "start to live again": be well dressed, well coiffed and perfumed, and sit in a café, having a drink or a coffee or go to a movie. There's nothing remarkable about a woman sitting alone in a bar in Buenos Aires, even at night.

It was a Friday; as usual, Federico's friends would gather at our house before going out dancing, and one of my reasons for leaving was to try to escape those hours of noise and disorder.

"Clean up after yourselves in the kitchen," I told Federico absent-mindedly on my way out.

I was absolutely insane. I had left the house in the hands of a group of adolescents, thinking I'd be able to enjoy some time alone in a café with a drink and a book. I went into a place on Avenida Corrientes, full of people, with a very congenial ambience and the noise of the espresso machine, which, far from annoying me, struck me as quite pleasant. As I removed my coat, I inhaled my own perfume; I had chosen a heavy fragrance, ideal for nighttime. There was no shortage of appreciative male glances at that petite woman, no longer young but still vivacious and well-turned-out, who I was at the moment. Looking at the skimpy bar menu, I studied the list of cocktails I recognized from my own adolescence: Cuba libre, manhattan, dry martini, or Saint Martin demi-sec, strawberry and pineapple fizz, made without alcohol for very young girls who would nonetheless grow up and blossom with the addition of gin; my all-time favorite, the Brandy Alexander, so innocent to look at because it contains sweet cream, yet so intoxicating. I never did drink much, but the first time I felt that wicked rush of alcohol in my body and in my head, I couldn't have been more than sixteen, and I wanted to imitate the grown-ups. As Omar Khayyám says on the El Abuelo port label, "Wine drunk in moderation lifts the spirits and warms the heart." That's the sort of drinker I've always been: I drank wine in moderation, except for the occasional slip, and I learned to appreciate what the Bols liqueur ads announced in old issues of *Caras y Caretas* magazine: "A glass a day." I never gave or received advice about overindulging: people who get drunk do so because they can't cope with this life – is it ever easy for anyone?

In any case cocktails are somewhat passé; now I see people drinking wine, whiskey, beer. I ordered a Saint Martin demi-sec for nostalgia's sake. A while later I was astonished to see the empty glass: I had drunk it very quickly. As I read, without retaining the meaning of a single sentence – I can't remember the name of the book I had brought along that night – I departed from custom and ordered another, diligently attempting to take very slow, tiny sips, but I didn't succeed. Soon I once again found myself before an empty glass, and I could hardly keep from looking at the clock; at last I had to peek. Only twenty minutes had gone by since I arrived. I suddenly had what seemed like a fantastic idea. Instead of going home early and facing the kids' racket, I could spend the rest of the night at a nearby hotel. I stood up quickly and had to grab the table with both hands. Only two drinks! I regained my balance right away and felt fine. I looked around to see if anyone had noticed my wooziness, but no one was looking at me. Federico's friends would just now be arriving, and all my efforts to escape them would go to waste if I returned home at that moment.

I'm familiar with hotels in many cities, in other parts of Argentina and in other countries, but just as it is with everyone else, the city where I know the fewest hotels is my own. My house is in Buenos Aires, so there's no reason for me to know about hotels, except for some very large, luxurious ones where other activities besides lodging people take place. But a small, reasonably priced hotel, where I might spend that night . . . I sat down again and called for the waiter to bring my check, while I kept thinking at full speed, calculating how much a room at the Claridge or the Alvear might cost. Luckily, I remembered a little hotel that would probably be acceptable and which was very close to the bar, a place where a French friend of mine used to stay whenever he came to Buenos Aires.

Suddenly I found myself in the street, with my coat on; I have no recollection of the waiter's coming over or of my paying the bill. I only know that the second time I stood up, I no longer felt perfectly fine: the bar, with its tables, the people, waiters passing with trays, all spun around before my eyes.

The hotel – what a great idea! I'd ask them to wake me at six a.m., and I'd return home. I left the bar trying to look confident and sophisticated. Out on the street the frozen air restored me to my austere condition of someone who doesn't usually get drunk. I took a taxi, arriving at the hotel in two or three minutes. But the taxi left me on the opposite side of the street, right in the middle of

Corrientes. I looked at the traffic on my left before crossing. I let two or three cars go by. I stepped off the curb and lost my balance again, even more than I had in the bar. I tried to take a step forward. Immediately I felt my arms being grabbed by strong hands. As though in a fog, I looked right and left; I couldn't believe my eyes. On either side of me was a policeman. What have I done? I thought.

One of them spoke: "That's not the way to cross the street, *señora*. Are you all right?"

I attempted to free my arms, but they wouldn't let me.

"Where are you going?"

"I'm going to that hotel across the street," I managed to reply. "I'm fine."

But they wouldn't let go; they crossed the street, escorting me to the entrance of the hotel, where, fortunately, no one was standing. How would I be able to ask for a room if they saw me walk in drunk, flanked by two cops? Once we arrived, they let go of me, tipping their caps and nodding slightly. I opened my mouth to say something, but no sound emerged. They left, and I walked in. The cold air had cleared my head. I walked up to the front desk.

Once inside my room (the cheapest one with a private bath), I discovered that the heat was meager. The room was so small that there was practically no space beside the double bed. I climbed into bed without taking off my clothes, just my coat, covered myself with the blankets, and opened my book. When I awoke two or three hours later, the book was lying on the floor open, face down. I hadn't turned off any of the lights, not even the overhead light, which illuminated the room in its full squalor. I went to the bathroom. The mirror on the medicine cabinet reflected a scraggly haired image with runny makeup. It was four o'clock in the morning. Less than a half-hour later I opened the door of my house with my key. Everything was silent. I assumed that Federico and his friends had left.

But they were still there. As soon as I closed the door, before turning on the light, a terrible odor, like stale smoke, alcohol, vomit, and sweat mixed with raspberry room deodorizer, hit me. I took a step forward, closed the front door, and headed for the window. I saw bodies lying, or rather sprawling, on the floor and in the armchairs. As I made my way toward the window, trying to step around them, I began to recognize other odors blended with that infernal stench: cat piss, dog shit, marijuana (the reason for the room deodorizer; one of them must have retained a bit of lucidity, enough to anticipate my return). I opened the window wide, and nobody moved or moaned; they seemed dead. I went into Federico's room. He was asleep in his bed with his shoes on; in the other twin bed two kids were sleeping head to foot, a boy and a girl.

Then I returned to the living room and began shouting and kicking the bodies surrounding me in the room, which was now completely illuminated and filled with the frigid, clean night air.

"Shit! Get up right now and clean up this mess! Let's go, move it!" And I mercilessly kicked ribs, shoulder blades, a face, a head. Someone let out a bloodcurdling cry as I stepped on his hand.

"Fuck it! Goddamn it! Clean all this up right now, you fucking pigs."

And all the while I was crying, and my heart was breaking for one of those poor creatures who had managed to sit up and was watching me from an armchair, his pupils dilated, uncomprehending. Like a bolt of lightning, the idea flashed through my mind of going over to him, hugging him, crying with him, and saying: "Baby, what's wrong? Come to Mama."

I realized it was useless to expect them to do anything, and I was exhausted. I kept on delivering kicks to those bodies until I managed to make them all get up and leave. One of them, slightly more awake than the rest, carried all the overcoats. Federico shouted from the hallway. I locked the door, returned to Federico's room, took his jacket and keys, opened the door, and threw them out. I dead-bolted the door so he couldn't get back in. Federico shouted for a long time, banging his fists against the door. Finally, I couldn't hear him anymore, and the house fell silent.

The next day he returned home, but his attitude worried me. He entered silently, not responding to my greeting. He followed me to my room and slumped onto the floor next to the bed. He remained like that, collapsed, his back against the wall. I said something to him, and he answered me, shouting in a way that surprised me: I had never heard him shout like that. But I wasn't afraid. The fear would come later.

Holding hands, Steve and I cross over to the little bakery where they sell those freshly baked croissants he loves. It's a wintry but sunny Sunday in Buenos Aires. As soon as we get back home, I'll make that coffee that's too strong for North Americans and barely colored water for Italians but which lies somewhere exactly in between, and we'll enjoy it together for what it is: one of life's great pleasures. I've taught Steve to dip his croissant in the *café con leche* as I've been doing for as long as I can remember, even in the most elegant pastry shops. Wasn't it a custom, at least for a while, to stir the ice cubes in your whiskey with your fingers? I don't think anyone does it anymore. I, for one (and now Steve, because he enjoys imitating me), dip bread in gravy; I take off my shoes at parties. I have pretty feet, and they're unblemished: Steve likes to rub them and feel them touching him between the sheets.

For our lunch today I'll make my chicken provençal, which certainly doesn't resemble what they make in Provence. In the Argentine version of chicken provençal you have to dredge the chicken parts in flour, brown them in oil or butter, and finish it off with fried onions and white wine (forgetting dietary proscriptions for a while); the potatoes are baked separately. The result should be crispy. While Steve reads the Sunday paper in the little winter garden that I made by closing off a sun-filled balcony with glass doors, the aroma of the cooking reaches him, and he comes into the kitchen as if drawn by a magnet, ready to help out however he can, like the well-trained North American man he is.

My last day in Buenos Aires. My stays at the spa are longer each time now, and the trips to my city seem like visits, but I can't stop feeling that "home" is my apartment in Buenos Aires. I look at my desk and my computer screen with a certain resentment. In order to describe things that caused me suffering, I have to suffer again, and even though it's a different kind of suffering, alleviated by simply getting up and leaving my work aside, I hesitate a few minutes before making up my mind. I go to the kitchen and make myself some coffee and toast. Finally, like an act of heroism, I sit down at the keyboard again.

Worn-out by the last year of Dardo's illness and his death and finding myself totally alone, I had to place some limits on Federico. The doctor explained how to do it. If he tried to impose his will by screaming me into submission, I was supposed to say these exact words to him: "No, I won't give you what you're asking me for. You may not realize it, you lazy slob, but if I don't keep this house together, no one will. In this house I'm the boss." That's what I said to him, word for word, when he asked me for money again, and that was the first time he hit me. We were in the living room, and his girlfriend (her name was Adelaida) was there. He demanded the money insolently, from the armchair where he was sprawled, as though I didn't deserve the effort it took him to open his mouth to ask. Immediately, I repeated to the comma the exact words the psychiatrist had dictated to me, concluding emphatically, "In this house I'm the boss."

That's not how it turned out. Federico stood up from the chair and came toward me like a tornado. In fact, he didn't really hit me. He delivered several strong shoves that propelled me through the room in a kind of epileptic dance. Terrified of falling to the floor at any moment or of banging my head on the corner of a piece of furniture, I managed only to beg, "Enough, Federico, enough!" before I found myself, God knows how, in front of the door to my bedroom. I went in, turned the key in the lock, and sat down on the bed, stunned, frightened, and trembling like a leaf.

Sometimes I wonder what it would have been like if Dardo hadn't died, because while it's true that he and I lost control of Federico when he was no more than a boy of thirteen or fourteen, only after Dardo's death did the unimaginable, the inconceivable, happen. Federico made scenes in the street; at home he shouted, frightening the neighbors; he broke things; he threatened me; he snatched my purse in order to steal money from me; he lied to me constantly; he manipulated me like a puppet; and he hit me many times. And I always drifted through that hell in a daze, unable to believe what was happening to me. I believed him when he said he was sorry, and I trusted it would never happen again. Pathological grief, I thought.

During Federico's increasingly frequent bouts of violence, I did many things for the first time in my life: calling the police, taking him to a hospital, fleeing from the house and seeking shelter with a friend, seriously risking my security, my resources, my right to be sad and my right to cry over Dardo's death. Everything except throwing Federico out on the street. There were several reasons for this: I didn't feel capable of doing it; besides, I considered his behavior a sickness, and when his tirades were over, I felt sorry for him. In my consultations with doctors, lawyers, and social workers, the reply was always the same: "You can't throw him out on the street, señora. It would be a crime. Federico is a minor. You have to give him love and limits."

Besides, who would have wanted to throw Federico out? When he calmed down, he was sorry and acted sweet and tender and bought me gifts with the money he had snatched from me earlier or stolen from me surreptitiously if I had forgotten to hide it in my bra.

Meanwhile, I continued to consult specialists. In general, they didn't consider the beatings too important. They asked me if Federico threw me on the floor and stomped me when he was hitting me, if he dragged me by the hair, if he'd caused me any serious injuries. I had to admit he hadn't, and then they quickly changed the subject. It was reassuring, after all, to know that Federico was a "normal" adolescent: all adolescents have crises, and during these crises they break whatever they can find, even their own belongings; they all throw the occasional piece of furniture out the window; all of them lie, threaten, steal; they all make suicide attempts that are generally a sham, like the scratches, sometimes bloody, that Federico made on his wrists. Two years later Federico's behavior would be classified as "normal behavior for drug-addicted youths."

All young drug addicts relapse, they said. They hide drugs, they run away from rehab centers or from home, and they come back as soon as they have to spend a night on a park bench.

In every house where a young addict lives, there's a broken door. This surprised me. Later I understood why there was a broken door. Behind that locked door was some poor human being – a mother, a wife with a baby in her arms – trembling with fear at the possibility of being beaten. They don't quite knock the door down, but they do make a hole in it that sometimes gets repaired right away and other times remains like that for a long time, a sign of the martyrdom someone has suffered.

Not everything can be blamed on drugs; there's also the addictive personality, of course (I don't know exactly what that is), and the addict's psychopathology. I have only a vague idea of what *psychopathology* means, but laymen can't know everything; we repeat what the professionals tell us, and it's no use desperately trying to figure out what "mistakes" we made in childrearing. Of course we made mistakes – who's ever prepared to be a father or mother? Just as Gypsies say our destiny is written in the palms of our hands, doctors say it's inscribed in our DNA. It's a modern form of fatalism.

You don't notice the circular movements unless you stare constantly through the glass walls. I'm with Steve in the revolving cocktail lounge on the twentieth floor of the San Conrado Building, from where the hang gliders jump. It's nighttime, and there are no hang gliders. When we face the sea, we can see the moon and its phosphorescence on the foamy crest of the waves. The cocktail lounge keeps revolving, and we see the dense darkness of the rainforest.

"They're microorganisms," Steve explains to me after we've made one complete rotation and the sea lies before us once more. "The phosphorescence is produced by microorganisms called *noctilucas*. He smiles at my absent-minded expression. I've never been too interested in science. Sometimes I feel I should care about it as much as he cares about what I write, but it's useless: anyone can read a novel, but very few nonspecialists read science, not even the popular magazines.

Steve's legs wrap around mine under the table. Everything's fine now. My own troubles and the troubles of all humankind fade; the surrounding world, including the rest of the lounge and the people surrounding us, also disappear into the background. The waiter comes over to the little table to serve the cocktails we've ordered, a dry martini for Steve and my invariable Brandy Alexander, and then withdraws.

"What are you thinking about?" Steve asks.

"I'll tell you later," I reply, seeking his hand on the tablecloth, a gesture more like grasping the edge of a cliff than a romantic touch. I'm a little afraid of my own pleasure. When I return to Buenos Aires, I tell myself, I'll make an appointment with my analyst and ask her if it's normal for a woman my age to:

surrender to love
with frenetic passion

as if I were fifteen or twenty years old, because I'm no longer twenty or thirty or even forty. Better not to go on. These are questions whose answers one knows, but psychoanalysts like it when their patients, who have suffered a lot and for a long time, show up one day with a radiant expression and a slightly timid gesture and confess that, right around the corner and when they least expected it, they found happiness again.

When I went to my first session, some time ago, I asked my analyst if she wanted me to lie down on the couch.

"Not at all," she said. "I need for you to be strong; you have a battle ahead of you."

I won the battle, certainly at a very high price, but I've never felt happy again, at least not that kind of happiness.

Steve raises his glass and makes a toast. "To the rainforest," he says.

"To the rainforest," I repeat.

We drink without releasing our hands. He starts to get up from his seat, and I do, too, and still holding hands we reach the small dance floor.

None of your laughter, you young people; this is very serious. It used to be called "slow dancing," and I suppose young people do it now, also, in addition to dancing alone or in trios or in large groups where each one does whatever he wants. They're a lovely sight, if you can stand the volume of the music. Music I'm not familiar with. I wonder if they've ever heard of Vinicius or Maria Creuza. These are the melodies Steve and I dance to.

In spite of the fact that customs were much more restrictive than they are now, in my youth other practices that allowed bodies to get closer to one another, besides slow dancing, which a girl could do with someone she didn't even know who had simply "asked her to dance," included embracing in the shadows of a deserted street lined with leafy trees or in the patios of houses. If those patios could talk, they would say things even more daring than what sofas could describe.

An embrace while dancing didn't leave any spaces: all parts of the body came in contact with the body of the other person, including cheek against cheek, and even the customary posture of extended arms with entwined hands could be abandoned in favor of a real embrace. Not even vigilant mothers, seated around the dance floor, could object.

But here there are no mothers, no young people. Only shadows, and a subtle blend of pleasant, nocturnal fragrances: perfume, alcohol.

I know I'll love you
all my life

sings Maria Creuza, and Steve presses me against him a little more. I rest my head on his chest (I don't even reach his shoulder) and allow myself to be carried away, my eyes closed.

We return to the table, holding hands, but now we sit in a leather booth at one side, next to each other, so we can kiss. I take a sip from Steve's glass, but he doesn't try my Brandy Alexander.

"That's formula," he says, even though I explain to him that in Spanish we don't say "formula" but, rather, "baby bottle" or "nursing bottle." Naturally, the whitish cocktail isn't baby pap; I already feel slightly woozy. Or maybe the waiter has replaced our empty glasses with full ones, responding to some gesture of Steve's that I hadn't noticed.

Another toast.

"To tonight," I say.

"To all the nights," Steve says.

I think of idiotic expressions like "eternity in this moment," but I don't say them. When we get up to dance again,

it only happens
when I dance with you

Steve's hand slides down from my waist to my sacrum. I don't know why it's called "sacrum," but it strikes me as a perfect description because when Steve's fingers run up and down there, I forget about everything; I only want this sacred ritual to continue. Steve understands. We never speak of this; it's something that doesn't need to be mentioned. Now, as we dance, and later, between the sheets, as dawn begins to light up the sky, in the hotel room in this very building.

Terror still seizes me in my dreams. I see Federico dead. I know I'm dreaming, and yet I don't want to resort to the system I use to wake myself whenever I realize I'm dreaming: moving my head from side to side, seeking contact with the pillow. Suddenly I find myself talking to my mother on the patio of the old house, and I know it's a dream because I remember that in reality she's dead. I don't generally like to talk to the dead in my dreams; when I wake up, I lose them again. It's like they died all over. Well, then, let them die as soon as possible, I tell myself. My dead mother says something to me in the dream, and I turn my head from side to side until I come in contact with the softness of the pillowcase, the nice warmth of the blankets, a vague, cool breeze filtering through the window. This dream is different because Federico is really alive, and I'm still there, in the street in my dream, watching my son splayed out under a tree, in the middle of a pile of garbage heaped next to the tree trunk. Federico has one eye closed and the other barely half-open. His body is stiff, on its side, his knees bent. He's wearing a dirty T-shirt and ripped jeans; his leg is still in a cast from a fracture he suffered playing soccer.

This time it's Steve's embrace that awakens me; he's still up. He's wearing his glasses and watching me very seriously. He hugs me; maybe he heard me moan in my sleep. For a change I don't feel bad when I awaken.

I harbored the hope that Federico would improve over time, with the help of psychotherapy, medication, and a young psychologist who was recommended to me when the situation became unbearable. The psychologist spent several hours a day at our house, usually in the afternoon. He was more like my bodyguard, but he operated under the more acceptable title of "therapeutic companion." Everything was conducted just as though he were a member of the family. When Federico was feeling all right, he chatted with him, and sometimes they holed up in Federico's room together. Whenever the companion was in the house, Federico didn't go out or invite anyone else over – no friends, no girlfriend – despite the fact that no one had specifically instructed him not to.

But the psychologist couldn't stay all day long, and Federico's violent outbursts continued whenever the therapist wasn't there.

Whenever Federico "got worse," I waited till he was asleep and escaped to a friend's house. I began to envy the owner of every house that sheltered me; their small apartments, their normal interaction with their children, struck me as an enormous luxury.

I took refuge in other people's homes whenever I needed to. I could make a long list of relatives' and friends' houses where I would suddenly show up with my bag to spend the night, or two or three nights, but I knew my presence was an inconvenience: I wasn't the sort of person that people cheerfully put up in their homes. I lugged my despair with me, and my delirium would erupt while we were having a drink together, pretending nothing was wrong with me. Temporarily getting away from Federico and his abuse made me feel momentarily euphoric.

Sometimes the euphoria showed up at inopportune times. One friend, uselessly trying to restrain himself, finally said: "Look, Cecilia, I know what's happening to you is terrible. Some other time you can come over with no problem, but this time I'd rather pay for a hotel room for you. Right around the corner from here, there's a pretty good one where we slept that night when we lost our keys – it was cheaper than paying a locksmith to pick the lock! You can't stay here tonight because I have to fight with my wife."

I took it all quite well, apparently.

"Please! There are thousands of places I can go! I'll just make a phone call, and I'll be on my way."

On that occasion I called Maia, a woman I hardly knew. She was more like a friend of a friend, and I'd never asked her if I could spend the night. She agreed enthusiastically right away; I had never been to her house before, and I knew she wanted to invite me. Maia was a woman of considerable physique, as Borges used to say. The contrast between me and these "considerable" women is remarkable. I look like Fellini's little Cabiria, wandering between those huge prostitutes. Maia was an ardent feminist, and I, whenever I could clear my mind of my own drama, also called myself one. We spoke about men and women's rights for a while. After a drink together, Maia resolved to make dinner. I followed her and was astonished: I had never seen such a dirty kitchen. Maia ill-humoredly swept aside the countless objects that covered the counter, especially dirty dishes with bits of leftover, hardened food stuck to them, unspeakably filthy dish towels, sugar that had spilled from the sugar bowl, which was lying on its side like the victim of some War of the Utensils. Somehow or other, she cleared a space, and without even the swipe of a sponge, she made some instant mashed potatoes and dumped them on the counter, added flour, cracked an egg, and beat it all up to make the dough, to which she added, without any compunction whatever, a significant portion of grime. I went to get myself some more whiskey in order to pluck up my courage, and when I returned to the kitchen, Maia was kneading the little balls of dough with a fork. We ate the gnocchi with a tasty reheated sauce from the day before. I ate eagerly, reassuring myself that heat kills bacteria. What right did I have to criticize her negligence when she was letting me stay in her house, I told myself.

Maia's son, a tall, dark boy who watched me suspiciously without speaking, ate with us, but while we were having coffee, he heard his mother say: "You can stay here as long as you like, Cecilia. As long as you like, no limit."

"Until I come back home to stay for a few weeks, Mom, while they're fixing up my place," the boy hurriedly said.

Maia winked at me, repeating: "All the time you like, Cecilia, no limit. My son can sleep in the guest room."

Then the boy got up and brusquely walked out. It was now obvious that I'd have to leave tomorrow at the latest.

I also stayed with Liliana, one of Maia's equally feminist friends, but as sparkling as a bubble. She had the kind of hands that seem to clean with a mind of their own, pursuing the last little stain with a detergent-soaked sponge. She lived very far from where I worked. After two or three days of traversing great distances by bus to teach my classes, I decided to go back home. In a very sweet voice Federico had told me on the phone that he was all right, that he had found another job as a pizza delivery boy, and that he had won his girlfriend back; his voice sounded calm and affectionate, and once again I believed that my hell had ended. I needed to believe it. In any case I had to leave my temporary refuge at Liliana's sooner than expected.

Liliana lived alone. We ate breakfast together, and I made it my business to provide packets of coffee and croissants; I washed the dishes, as if doing that could compensate for my unexpected presence. But one morning Liliana, who had returned home very late the night before, emerged from her bedroom in a nightgown, closing the door carefully behind her, and joined me in the kitchen. I'd put the water on to boil; Liliana, with a sour expression, barely responded to my greeting and announced that she would have breakfast in bed. She put two cups and two dishes, two pieces of toast and two croissants, on a tray, and I understood: there was someone with her in the bedroom. She had every right, didn't she? She was in her own house. She went into the bedroom with the tray and closed the door carefully again. I could hear the ominous click of the key in the lock. One minute later I was gathering my things, and I tiptoed out of the house. In my head, which felt like it was stuffed with cotton, the first lines of an old anarchist song echoed:

I'm nothing but a stray,
What I have, I sell or give away . . .

During one of my last "escapes," Federico pretended to attempt suicide in a different way: instead of scratching his wrists with a razor blade, he made lots of scratches on his belly. Yet another girlfriend had left him. Who wouldn't have, when he kept abusing them? They withstood the insults and blows while Federico was seducing them, and they left for good when it was no longer worth the effort. I let two whole days go by without communicating with him. When I phoned him from my temporary refuge, he cried for help: "Mama! Mama!"

I went upstairs to the apartment with the therapeutic companion, a doctor, and an emergency room nurse. Sebastián, a brand-new physician who was doing his residency in the hospital, also waited for me at the door, and together we all managed to take Federico to an observation room. While we waited, I told the story. A policeman put his arm around Federico, saying, "I was once eighteen, too, Federico; my girlfriend left me, too . . ."

Federico had a special talent for rewarding himself for things he hadn't done: confident of my incredible meekness, for several months he forced me to make prepayments for a "graduation trip" for the students who finish high school, and he simply went along with the real graduates without even having completed his sophomore year. The sponsoring organization was sending the kids to a hotel in Bariloche, with rooms with a private bath. A room with a private bath for a boy who should have been camping with a backpack! I was supposed to make the prepayments to an office downtown, even though it frightened me to think that Federico had repeated his first year and had gone through the second year twice without passing.

"There are other kids who didn't graduate, and they're going on the graduation trip, anyway," Federico assured me.

But he didn't say it pleasantly. He glared at me with hatred-filled eyes, made a threatening gesture, and pushed me out of his room.

He managed to say (and I managed to believe) that if I didn't let him go on that trip, he'd set the house on fire.

Violence has been part of my life for as long as I can remember, and not just in my family. I was just a little girl when I heard a man shout from behind a partition wall, "I'm going to burn the place down!" I was on the patio, paralyzed with fear, but I wasn't alone in the house; my elders had certainly heard, too, but kept silent. Did they think that was the best way to protect me? Did they think my five-year-old ears couldn't understand that tragic cry? I didn't say anything, either. If no one spoke about that, it must be because you weren't supposed to.

I put up with everything Federico dished out as long as he didn't become violent. Since I couldn't work at home, I taught classes in other people's houses, traveling through Buenos Aires by bus. We lived on my earnings from teaching because I didn't want to exhaust my meager remaining resources, having lost nearly everything with Dardo's illness, and what I earned didn't bring in too much. I went out in the afternoons, from one house to another, gathering strength from who knows where in order to seem enthusiastic and cheerful as I taught, although the pills made me nauseated and very drowsy.

One of my students was a special woman, quite reserved, who said very little about herself. Once when I arrived late because of some kind of domestic crisis, I briefly told her I'd been having problems with my son. Teenage stuff, I told her. Teenagers are awful, she replied, as I expected. But from that day on she always asked me about him.

She was taking classes to improve her English. At a given moment she invariably got up to make coffee, and I went to the bathroom, a small, coquettishly decorated toilette, where I avoided looking at myself in the mirror in order not to see what the ravages of the day before had done to my face. A few minutes later we would continue, and that was the hardest part because I felt my eyelids closing as though they were made of lead. Until one day, when we had resumed our work after having coffee, I suddenly heard my student say in a slightly louder than normal voice, "Um, um . . ." I woke up with a start and kept talking as if nothing had happened, pretending the impossible: that I hadn't fallen asleep. We said good-bye as usual, and a few days later I showed up to give the next class. She let me teach as usual, and when I went to the bathroom, I prayed to that God whom I sometimes believe in to keep me awake until the end. Finally, a furtive glance at my watch revealed that it was time to go. I stood up to say good-bye, and she said, with the same serious, blank expression as always, that she was going to take some time off from classes while she had the house remodeled. That's how she dismissed me, summarily, like a clerk or a maid whom one allows to work without saying anything until the last minute so that she won't botch up some document or spit in the coffee.

During one of those wanderings from house to house, I caught a glimpse of myself in the window of a large bookstore, where I had stopped to look for something. Was that me? Incredibly thin (a million diets all my life had never left me like that) and with a face unhinged by anguish. I went into the old café at the corner of Las Heras and Pueyrredón to rest for a few minutes and left my coffee untouched. The students that afternoon were a group of nine-year-olds. They were always mischievous, but that day they did unprecedented things. I had turned around for a moment to point out something in the video we were watching, and when I turned back to face them again, I discovered that one had disappeared, another was watching me from the top of a staircase, precariously balanced over the banister, while yet another was standing on his head, repeating the phrase we had just learned. I screamed at them for the first time. The grandmother of the boy whose house we were in came running, and I told her, smiling, that we were practicing a dialogue. She calmed down and went to look for a tray with soda and candy for the kids and some coffee for me.

At night, in the darkness of my room as I tried to sleep, I was assailed by the fear of finding myself sitting on the subway stairs, exhausted, ragged, and holding out a tremulous hand to passersby, with my head wrapped in a kerchief like the ones beggar women use, both real beggars and those who dress the part.

In Bologna I once saw a woman sitting in the middle of a café, begging, with a clown's painted face and false nose. I thought she was an actress, asking for money for some theater. Someone explained to me that in that noble city they practiced an old custom: people disguised themselves in order to hide their identity and their shame. Those regal beggars are known as "i poveri vergognosi." Me, a *povera vergognosa*! Exploited and beaten by my own son, trembling at his screams! Whenever the image of the beggar woman struck me, I turned on the light and swallowed half an extra pink pill in order to fall asleep. In the morning when I awoke, I ran to see if the money that I'd hidden between the pages of a book the previous afternoon was still there.

One afternoon I was in my bedroom when Federico entered, very composed and with a sad expression, inviting me to his room because he needed to talk to me. That day the therapeutic companion hadn't come, and Federico took advantage of his absence to invite his girlfriend, Adelaida. I found her in Federico's bed, her eyes veiled with sleep and hung over from the night before. She didn't rush to get up when she saw me enter or even try to get out of bed. It was four o'clock. Sitting at the edge of the bed, Federico told me he had a confession to make: she was pregnant. The girl followed him with the expression of a cow being taken to slaughter: since it doesn't understand, it doesn't care. They had decided, Federico continued, that she should have an abortion because they were both very young and had to study and work (a utopian vision, by any standard), and having a baby would be foolish under those conditions. My hesitant expression alone at this revelation was enough to ignite the fury in Federico's eyes. I hurriedly told him I would give them the money even before they asked me for it.

Adelaida was the same age as Federico; she was tiny, contrasting dramatically with his corpulence. And now, in the absence of the therapeutic companion, Federico was beating her before my eyes. I was afraid even to move. I stood next to the table, not looking at them.

For two or three weeks I had innocently waited for them to use the money for the announced purpose. Although I tried to conceal it, I lived in constant fear that Federico's fury would be unleashed against Adelaida or against me. Like now.

After beating her until she lay flat on the floor, Federico seemed to calm down. I didn't look at him; I just spoke to him in measured tones, like to a small child. "You can't hit Adelaida, Federico," I said. "You can't hit a woman, and besides, she's pregnant."

I didn't see him coming toward me. Suddenly I felt his fist against my face.

My eyeglasses flew through the air; my nose swelled. After a moment of stupefaction, I got down from the table, picked up my glasses, escaped to my room running, and burst out crying while sitting in a chair. I cried meekly, occasionally touching my swollen nose. Later Federico and Adelaida came in with a bouquet of flowers. I had put some ice cubes in a plastic bag and was applying it to my nose. They approached; they spoke to me sweetly. Federico swore it would never happen again.

"I got upset because you told me I couldn't hit Adelaida," he explained.

They were going to get jobs so they could help me, he said; all three of us would be very happy. Adelaida had no visible marks from the beating; she had washed her face, and her shiny black hair was gathered in an elastic band at the back of her neck.

The following Monday, when I summoned the nerve to go out in the street with dark glasses, the swelling had gone down, but I had traces of black-and-blue under my eyes. No one asked me anything; if I happened to meet an acquaintance, I quickly said that I had bumped into a window in the dark.

Battered women are usually victims of their husbands or boy-friends, and as certain North American TV movies illustrate, it's hard for them to overcome the problem because they're more afraid of being alone than of living with someone who mistreats them or because they believe they deserve to be abused. I wasn't beaten by my husband or my boyfriend (in any case I had neither); I was beaten by my son.

At the Battered Women's Center they told me I needed to scream. And that only during an attack could I call for help from the police or other institutions, because witnesses were required, proof. As if that were possible. When he attacked me, Federico would lock me in my bedroom, disconnect the phone, and hide the house keys.

I also sought help from many private institutions and profes-sionals, some of them quite expensive. I always left bearing some distressing picture of those psychiatric hospitals, like a souvenir. They attended to me in the adolescent section, but in order to get there, more than once I had to go through the adult wing: through the barred windows I could see the pale faces of those who had to be locked up because they were a danger to themselves and to others. Sometimes I would pass through a ward of patients who were con-fined to bed. They weren't sick of body, but of soul, some of them drowsy from medication or from depression. You had to be strong to look at those defeated creatures without bursting into tears. It could happen to anyone, I thought, anyone at all.

Adelaida was talking to a girlfriend. She was talking on my phone in my living room, very close to me, as I listened indifferently. She was telling her friend that she was pregnant and that being pregnant was beautiful. (It was beautiful, all right, and she was going to have an abortion with the money I had given her.)

Adelaida wanted to break up with Federico. And he beat her so she wouldn't leave him. Strange, isn't it? Especially since the blows were effective. Adelaida declared in my presence to one of the many psychiatrists we consulted that she wouldn't leave Federico even though he hit her. Finally, one night, when she was four months pregnant, Federico and a friend took her to a clinic in the suburbs, where she had an abortion.

What if I were a clown, an actress, a teller of horror stories? What if none of this ever really happened? Limits, *señora*, you have to give him limits. Federico is a minor; you can't throw him out on the street; you have to give him love, and at the same time you need to be firm with him. But he smashes me against the wall, I tell them; he grabs my purse and empties it out on the floor before my eyes and steals whatever he finds; I have to hide the money.

Around that time I unexpectedly received some money that bolstered my afflicted savings. Federico found out about the windfall and proposed that I give him part of it so he could open a snack bar. And that I should be his partner. I couldn't help laughing a little, and I said no. He became enraged. I felt weakness in my body, my arms and legs, the urgent need to go lie down. Controlled by fear, and in order to make him change the subject and forget the idea of the "business" and of my being his partner, I offered him an absolutely ridiculous sum for an eighteen-year-old boy, and we went to the bank to make the withdrawal. In the taxi I thought: when I go down to the basement to get the dollars out of the safe-deposit box and he has to wait upstairs, I'll ask the bank clerks to call the police. I'll tell them: the boy who's waiting for me upstairs is my son. My son beats me; he's threatened me and forced me to come here to withdraw the money and give it to him.

Naturally, I didn't dare. It was all too unbelievable. I withdrew the money. In my dazed state I thought: "There's still plenty left. Why not give him part of it to see if he'll be reasonable?" I no longer felt afraid. I opened the safe-deposit box and took out the dollars, put them in my purse, handed the key back, and went upstairs. Federico was waiting for me; some employees and the security guard were watching us carefully. I tried to appear composed, but I was trembling, and Federico's eyes fired evil sparks.

Of course, Federico didn't use that money for one single useful purpose, despite the fact that he said he would spend it on musical equipment for a gig as a disc jockey. He bought himself clothing, an expensive leather jacket that was later "stolen" from him (he had, in fact, exchanged it for drugs) and designer sunglasses; he tried to put a down payment on a motorcycle, expecting me to pay the rest. I don't know how, but I refused, recovered some of my strength, and threatened to call the police.

He fixed his eyes (or rather his sunglasses) on me, looking as though he was about to spit at me, then turned and went to his room. Those sunglasses made me wonder, just as the room deodorizer did. Why did Federico use them so often, I asked myself like an idiot and immediately turned my thoughts to other things.

Federico also bought himself a baseball bat without ever having played baseball. He explained that it was for protection from neighborhood thugs.

The pretense that my son's problems were ordinary teenage troubles flew right out the window. When he threatened the therapeutic companion with the baseball bat, the psychologist decided to bring a gun on his next visit. Of course he'd never use it against Federico, he told me, but it would give him a scare.

For my part I had already made up my mind to run away for good.

The day of my move Federico was in very bad shape. He wasn't sad that I was leaving; he was furious. Like a robot, I gathered some essential things in a suitcase and filled two baskets with clothing and books. I left everything else for Federico. Furniture, kitchen items, many books that I couldn't take with me and would never read again, the tea glasses that Dardo's mother, Berta, had brought from Russia, with their carved metal holders, part of a modest but treasured early inheritance that she had given Dardo and me when she began to feel her time in this world was running out.

With my departure Federico lost the magic wellspring that he could immediately turn on every time he demanded something. The therapeutic companion helped me carry the baskets into the hallway. We were waiting for the elevator when Federico appeared at the door, wielding the baseball bat. Just as he had announced, the psychologist pulled out the pistol and fired two shots into the air. The shots caused a real panic among the neighbors in the building: they were fired at the front door of our apartment, and everyone heard them. When we reached the street, I heard the voice of a desperate woman, a pleasant person whom I used to chat with whenever we met in the elevator, shouting my name over the intercom. Neither the therapeutic companion nor I responded, and the driver swiftly loaded my bundles into his moving van.

And thus ended forever my son's violence against me, if for no other reason than because the opportunity to exercise it had ceased. Federico had found his limits at last.

The movers unloaded my things, and I was alone in my new residence. I didn't sense the joy of freedom. I sensed the smell of death. Nevertheless, sometime after settling in to the apartment, I discovered the good acoustics of the three-by-three-foot hall outside the bathroom. Suddenly I started to sing again; I couldn't remember how long it had been since I last sang. I have a thin but very well-pitched voice that allowed me to sing in a choir as a girl or just to sing for my own pleasure. I sang in the shower and emerged from the bathroom singing, wrapped in a bath towel and with another towel wrapped around my head like a turban. My voice sounded very good in the hall:

Andalusians of Jaén,
You haughty olive pickers,
Tell me true, whose olive trees are these,
Whose olive trees are these,
Andalusians of Jaén,
Andalusians of Jaén . . .

I liked the mantra of "Andalusians of Jaén"; it let me shed my son, who seemed prepared to strip me of everything I possessed: money, objects, my self-respect, peace, sleep. He had become the owner of the olive groves, and I was the hired hand.

I had moved once again, but this time without Federico. That dark, one-room apartment suited me perfectly. In truth, with a little more time and patience I might have found something much nicer for the same price. I rented it without thinking of anything other than escape. But its single window faced a "well of air and light" (the expression has always seemed odd to me, like the exit of a mine shaft that keeps the miners from suffocating), from which shouts, annoying music, babies crying, and cooking odors emanated. Day and night I had to turn on the lamp in order to work; whenever there was a power outage (and that summer there were several), I wrote by hand in a notebook resting on the windowsill.

I was starting over, like so many other times in my life and as though I were as young as before: a girl who leaves home, searching for independence. I attempted to recreate my bohemian days of decades ago; I furnished the little kitchen with trinkets I bought in the hardware store across the street. I even managed to invite friends over (never more than two or three at a time because they'd have nowhere to sit). Just like my students, they sat on the sofa bed where I slept. My books and papers continued to accumulate as usual, and there was no place to set up a new library.

I was no less troubled than before, but only now, without blows or threats, could I begin to recover. All the inconveniences were nothing compared to the pleasure of feeling like the owner of the olive groves.

I'm jolted awake by the buzzer of the alarm clock that I myself set to remind me that at seven Steve and I are going out for a walk and then to dinner. I look around, somewhat surprised at no longer being in that dark apartment where I once sampled the taste of freedom regained.

Now I live in a spacious, light-filled apartment. In winter, when it's dark by six, and whenever the sky is clear, an extraordinary phenomenon takes place: a false sunset in my living room. The sun beams in through the window, something that couldn't happen naturally because of the direction in which the building faces. There's a blinding mirrored window on a building across the street. That window projects the sun like an accidental gift as it filters in during the afternoon. I hurry to shower and dress; Steve's spent the afternoon taking pictures in La Boca and Barracas, and he'll be here any minute. Tomorrow we return to the spa.

Tenuous light and first shadows.

I'm worried about changes in my relationship with Steve. "My relationship with Steve" just slipped out; it's one of the expressions that's bounced about by the vulgarization of psychotherapy and which I hate, just like when I hear someone say, "My partner wants us to go to the seashore this summer." (Who is that sexless, nameless, faceless person called "my partner"?). A female friend announced, right in the middle of Café Ideal on Suipacha: "Look, Cecilia, here comes my partner." And I was astonished to see a normal, pleasant man approaching.

But what really worries me is that, almost without realizing it, I've gotten myself into this new situation: we no longer live in the little hotel spa (although we haven't disconnected ourselves from the treatment) but, rather, in the twenty-story tower in San Conrado, overlooking the sea. I'm making progress toward a normal life, without medical supervision, but I'm afraid to be under Steve's loving protection only to lose it later. It's true that I'm beginning to feel as though the suite we occupy in the hotel is my home, at least for a while, and that living with Steve doesn't force me to sacrifice anything. In the suite I have a study, much more luxurious than the ones I had in my various Buenos Aires apartments, although I still haven't brought the *Femminismo* poster or the cardboard Pierrot. Through the window I can see the ocean, on brilliant days, cloudy days, or in the midst of colossal storms.

At last I can continue to write here while Steve flies his hang glider through the clear skies (sometimes he passes by my window and waves to me) or travels to Los Angeles or anywhere else in the world. Here, when he's not around, I can give vent to my sadness and cry for the son I've lost. There's no love that can make up for the loss of a child. Who knows, who knows, I keep telling myself. Maybe one day Federico . . .

Here in San Conrado we receive *O Globo* and a Buenos Aires newspaper. It was in the Argentine paper this morning that I discovered something unsettling; in the home supplement section, among stories about décor, pets, and recipes, I read the story of a dog that helped an old lady recover, a woman so sick and so depressed that she didn't want to go on living. I was staring at the ceiling when the timer on the toaster went off and the toast jumped out, startling me. I spread it with soft cheese and orange marmalade, poured myself some steaming coffee from the coffeemaker, and returned to the newspaper. On the other half of the page there were classified ads. I read the categories: Personal assistant. Dressmakers, tailors, and alterations. Security guards, astrology, and Tarot. Matrimonial agencies. Companions. The last few sounded promising.

Female lawyer, 5'6", brunette, green eyes, feminine, athletic, and independent, looking for a serious relationship.

An agency called Just Love offered Hebrew Introductions, offering VIP types, warmth, and status.

I went on to the next category: Companions. I immediately thought of the therapeutic companion from my last days with Federico, but a single glance at the ads made me smile.

They offered:

April, a Paraguayan goddess, twenty-two, passionate and "all woman."

Annette, an innocent young girl, freshman, passionate and all woman (I wondered what was missing from those who weren't "all woman").

Ana was a Russian masseuse from San Isidro.

Axel, who was hot-blooded and loved to party, was waiting for me. Followed by a Flores telephone exchange.

Facundo, twenty-one, irresistible and well built, offered VIP pleasure and vice.

Rico, very well built . . . (Here I stopped to think: were these well-built young guys waiting for me, with my shocking lack of youth and my wrinkles, or were they waiting for some man my age? Or whichever of the two of us would pay them?).

Giselle, a heart-stopping brunette from Caballito, offered privacy in her own home.

Ivana was an excellent gaysha (exact spelling).

Sandy was a sweet fat girl, and Suki a very friendly, exotic Japanese lady.

I set the paper aside and went over to the window. Steve was probably flying somewhere in the area, but I didn't spot him. Suddenly I trembled. I just remembered that I had found the paper open to that page. What had Steve been reading? The story of the old lady and the little dog? The list of companions to call on our next trip to Buenos Aires?

We had lunch on the terrace of our suite, a brochette of enormous shrimp and then some slightly dry beef, and I didn't respond to his questions about why I wasn't smiling. After coffee the waiter removed the cups and the tablecloth. Steve took my hand, and we went into the bedroom. When he closed the curtains, we were in nearly total darkness, which he mitigated by lighting a small table lamp. He embraced me, gazing at me with moist eyes. I had one last thought: the image of a toothless, hundred-year-old Indian woman on the cover of *National Geographic*. Isn't that how I would look to him, compared to the twenty-two-year-old Paraguayan? But by then our bodies were already touching the sheets, and I stopped thinking.

"What do you know about your son and drugs?" the psychiatrist asked me.

It was a group meeting to which Federico himself had summoned me.

"Well," I said, "I figured that, besides getting drunk, he sometimes smokes a joint."

"Marijuana is a drug, and alcohol is also a drug," the doctor replied, dryly. "Now you say something, Federico."

"I also do cocaine," my son said.

I was nailed to my chair, facing the doctor. I don't recall what else the doctor said during the meeting, except, of course, that Federico needed treatment. We were in the office for less than fifteen minutes. A secretary gave me an appointment card for Federico to see the psychiatrist a week later. Then they called to notify me that the appointment would be postponed for another week because the psychiatrist had to attend a meeting. When we finally returned to the hospital, they made us wait a half-hour, and Federico was in the doctor's office for exactly fifteen minutes.

Two days later, on Saturday, the telephone woke me at three a.m. Federico, crying, asked me to meet him because he had started drinking and using cocaine again, and he couldn't bear the solitary torture that followed. As I had forbidden him to come to my house, we met at a bar. I had to buy him a beer, he told me, to get rid of the terrible depression. I watched the bottle being placed on the table, and I heard Federico, more composed now after his first drink, swear that this would be the last time he got high.

A little later, when the absolute uselessness of the eyedropper treatment suggested by the hospital's prepaid medical plan had been confirmed (it took me longer to fill out a complex form, sign it, and verify my signature every time I went in with Federico than the fifteen minutes he spent with the doctor), a friend told me about a rehab center for drug dependency, and we arranged our first appointment.

Periodically, I visited my old apartment, where Federico continued to live in chaos; I checked his phone calls, carefully inspected all the nooks that could be hiding places for drugs, observed his behavior, his facial expressions. After all was said and done, I was still a victim of his whims: he continued to drink and do drugs on weekends, interrupting my sleep with his calls. Early one morning I received a call from the police station. The police superintendent and I agreed that Federico would spend the night there and I would pick him up the next morning. At exactly eight o'clock they "released" him to me. I gave fifty pesos to the young officers who had treated him well, and the two of us left the police station in silence. Dawn had broken, and Federico saw an open bakery on the opposite sidewalk. We crossed to buy croissants for breakfast.

When he finally agreed to check into Lezama Clinic (they convinced him by telling him it would only be for a month), Federico had a black eye and a deep cut over his left eyebrow, the result of a punch delivered by his ex-girlfriend's father; he had acquired the habit of standing in front of her house at all hours of the night, shouting wildly at her to come outside.

The Rehabilitation Center for Drug Dependency known as Lezama Center is located in Constitución, opposite the park, surrounded by beautiful, European-style buildings and wide, tree-lined streets, a reminder that the neighborhood was once wealthy. The parents of the young patients are invited to participate in the group session, meeting once a week with a psychologist to deal with their common problem. Some attend only occasionally, others never, like one alcoholic mother and a father who didn't want to see his ex-wife. There are also absent parents, dead parents. Everyone is a little bit ashamed of their addicted children (it's taken a long time – even years – for most of them to figure out that their children take drugs), but they harbor a great deal of hope, despite the fact that they echo, like parrots, whatever they're taught there: drug addiction is incurable, but addicts can recover, and the signs of that recovery are clear: they go back to school; they find a job and keep it; they want to become independent of their families. But why, why?

Why did they get into drugs in the first place? The psychologist talks about personalities with addictive tendencies; addicts have weaker personalities, in spite of the violence they're capable of demonstrating, which their siblings, for example, don't demonstrate.

Donald, Steve's son, is also an addict, but he has a different sort of personality. Donald, unlike Federico, can't handle being alone without attention and can't get by on his own. Sometimes they commit him to an institution; sometimes he lives with his mother. He, too, becomes aggressive, but like a baby he depends on his parents, who have been separated for years. Steve also has two other easygoing, studious children, whom he hardly ever talks about.

Steve is the only person in the spa whose story I know. Who can tell? Maybe those reserved Finns are also the parents of addicts; getting us all together in the same place could make it easier for our caretakers to treat us. But I'm not too interested in finding out. And less interested still in attending group sessions. My God! For forty years, on and off, I've been a member of some group or other with common problems. Psychotherapy groups, Diet Club groups, relaxation groups, French language reading groups, groups for parents of drug addicts. Just hearing the word *group* makes me nauseous.

The Lezama Center operated in an enormous "sausage" house, of which there are still many examples in Buenos Aires: entryway, front hall, screen door, stained glass panels separating the parlor from the patio, which faced two other large rooms, one of which also looked out onto the street, with a balcony from which many young patients leaped to the street in order to escape, although they generally returned. It was a fairly new institution, considered "soft" in terms of the discipline imposed on patients. In all these centers there are disciplinary measures used for those who violate the rules, but they don't call them that, and certainly not "punishments."

At Lezama they called them "educational measures" or simply "educationals." Federico would let me know by phone: "This weekend I can't leave because they gave me an educational." I found out about a punishment that was applied in another, "harder" center: it consisted of scraping stains off a vast wooden floor with a penknife.

During the entire duration of the educational the person being disciplined couldn't eat or drink or talk to anyone else. At Lezama things seemed more humane: if someone committed an infraction, he had to wash all the dishes for a week (I calculated there were approximately three hundred dishes, considering how many people ate there and counting only one dish per person for each of the three main meals).

The young patients slept two or three to a room, in simple but pleasant quarters. In order to combat depression, they were always kept busy with something, and they weren't allowed to stay in their rooms during the day. The inpatients were almost all male; the only girl in the group was an outpatient whose mother punctually picked her up at seven in the evening. The patients ranged between seventeen and thirty years of age, and they all had to obey the Center's rules: alcohol and drugs strictly forbidden and no sex, either. They weren't even allowed condoms to avoid AIDS and pregnancy.

Every two weeks they held a barbecue for the patients' families, and music was allowed, as long as it didn't sing the praises of drugs. The young people danced, and someone watched them to make sure that couples didn't lock themselves in the bedrooms, in the naive belief that you can copulate only in bed.

At Lezama I found out how Federico managed to obtain drugs, even when he could no longer extract money from me: he offered other people the apartment I was paying for, where he lived until he was hospitalized, as a hideout in exchange for a few lines of cocaine.

"I need a lawyer," he told me one day in an imperious voice on the telephone. "I got a court order . . . or something like that. The management is complaining that they hear a lot of noise coming from my apartment. What assholes."

At the parents' meeting I learned the words *snow, White Lady, to score*. To score is to ask unsuspecting people walking down the street for a peso "for the bus"; the one who asks isn't a beggar; he's a polite, middle-class boy in designer jeans and shoes who claims not to have any money for the ticket. And I learned what being strung out means.

When I went to visit Federico once a week, they would call him, and he nearly always received me nicely, unless he was very depressed. Sometimes he hugged me and burst out crying. All these young people have moments of great tenderness and self-loathing when they weep in the arms of their parents, their psychologists, the ex-addicts who facilitate the groups.

All the fathers and mothers in the group would tremble whenever someone relapsed or ran away or had to start again from scratch, if by some good fortune he decided to return to the Center.

At times Federico seemed to be making progress; he showed up wearing the immaculate sports clothes I'd bought him, designer sneakers, and the Scottish soccer shirt he wanted and which I'd brought back for him from one of my trips. That perfect boy, alcohol and drug free, smiled at me, hugged me, and kissed me. We made plans for him to attend cooking school or to study hotel management. He wanted to win Adelaida back.

Two days later a familiar crisis exploded.

Federico was now twenty-two; he was legally an adult. When he was admitted to the Center, I stopped paying rent on his apartment, after paying for a broken door, and I refused to admit him into my home: if he ran away from Lezama, his only alternative would be the street.

"Listen, it would be better for you to go back to the Center," I told him when he called, holding the telephone in one hand and with the other rummaging around in the desk drawer for the pink pill.

The palpitations had already begun. My doctor had told me that now I had to look after my own needs first. I hung up. Later I called the Center, and they told me all we could do was to wait for him to come back. He had no money; he hadn't taken anything. Two hours later I phoned again, and he had, in fact, returned. They allowed him to speak to me. He cried, saying that Adelaida had left him.

It frightens me terribly to be with Steve and realize how much we like each other. I was going to say "love each other," but that frightens me even more. What if he gets sick and dies, like Dardo? We've talked about that.

"It's true," he replied. "I could get sick and die, like Dardo."

When I heard him repeat it, without a trace of anger or fear, just seriously and sadly, I thought, sometimes North Americans are remarkable, the way they're trained to discuss a fatal diagnosis soberly, to talk about how much time they have left. At least that's how it is with Steve and with movie characters. Right now Steve's an athlete, but he could go hang gliding one morning and die in his sleep that same night. Can anyone swear to me this will never happen?

"It's also possible I might get sick and die first," I said.

Steve remained silent for a few seconds and then tickled me. I can't stand being tickled, but I couldn't stop him from doing it. I was talking about serious stuff, and it was no time for fooling around. But I could not, nor did I want to, prevent a sensuality I thought I had lost from returning.

Now, as Steve surrenders to sun, sky, and sea, I peek out the window of the study in my hotel suite from time to time in order to watch him. I take a ream of printing paper from my desk drawer and discover, shuffled together with the ream, a few sheets with the Ministry of Culture letterhead.

I had accepted that proposal without thinking twice. The phone call from the secretary of culture had come at an opportune time, because my reserves were drying up. One has to live somehow, I told myself. One afternoon I chatted with him in his office, sitting on the other side of his desk, leaning against the back of the chair. I couldn't believe what was happening to me: I felt about as prepared to be a literary bureaucrat as an astronaut. There are much more serious problems to solve than those concerning culture in this country and in the world, and this example should suffice: any middle-class person (a writer, for example) walking down Avenida Corrientes on her way to a movie theater or a bookstore has to dodge panhandlers and see street kids begging. And the writer thinks about society, about gradual reforms, about bloody revolutions, about solidarity, about world hunger. Later, however, just as planned, she goes to see a movie or walks into a bookstore.

In my new workplace no one knew about the seriousness of my personal problems, and if anyone suspected, they were very careful not to ask questions. I understand that, and in their place I'd have done the same thing. Everyone has his own problems, pains. I was surprised when they called me back a few days later to ask what I'd decided. I thought I had clearly said yes, that I'd accepted.

My tasks were simple. One consisted of representing the authorities at official meetings, lectures, book presentations, awarding of prizes, roundtables, poetry readings, places my colleagues and I normally frequent, in order to keep our names and faces visible and to earn a few more pesos.

And so I embarked upon my new job in the Ministry of Culture, and without realizing it, I began to feel that the stately (although quite run-down) building where I had my office was also my home. At first the responsibility made me nervous, but I got used to it. It's a matter of smiling discreetly while the people who've requested appointments present their projects, and it's a foregone conclusion that the government has no money to finance them. Conversing casually with ambassadors, with ministers; forgetting about one's own family saga of embarrassing paupers who came to America; and evoking a mythical, splendorous past back in Europe.

I fulfilled the tasks assigned to me. I enjoyed traveling as a Ministry employee, and I freed myself from Federico's persecution for a few days at a time. I went to Tucumán, Mendoza, Trelew, Río Gallegos, Bariloche, the Pampa with its siestas – dangerously sad if one stays in one's hotel room, suicidal if one goes out walking through the deserted, treeless streets of Santa Rosa. I went to Posadas, Rosario and Santa Fe, Córdoba, Paraná, Concordia, Gualeguaychú, Bahía

Blanca, Puerto Madryn, Río Gallegos, and to provincial towns where they held book fairs, almost devoid of books, and where nearly all the residents claimed to be writers.

In my suitcase I carried quite a few books, self-published ones, with just a few short poems and lots of white space. I envied the passion of a literature professor from El Chaco and her students, who brought wine and *empanadas* to sample after class. At that time the government still had some money to pay hired artists and writers, and I enjoyed a relatively tranquil life, except for Federico's volcanic eruptions (now all by phone). In that Versailles-like mansion (although the ground floor was the only place that retained a certain decadent dignity, with its moth-eaten tapestries and screens and the curtains that had darkened from white to mouse-gray and then directly to black), I worked in a tiny office, where people who had come to see me congregated, and every morning an officious waiter who looked like a distant, very poor relative of Anthony Hopkins came in. Without losing his air of regal servitude, this man periodically collected money from us to buy coffee and sugar.

Federico showed up at the Ministry without prior notice. He made friends with the policewoman at the reception desk.

I spoke with her, briefly alerting her about what was going on and asking her not to let him in.

"*Señora*," she said with teary eyes, "I have a son myself. Don't ask me to shut the door on that boy."

I kept silent. What can you do about a mother's feelings? Federico, pale and garrulous, introduced himself and soon had the policewoman right in his pocket, just as he had done before with doctors, psychologists, social workers, and anyone who didn't really know the story. In fact, practically nobody knew the story because even though I might relate one episode, it was practically impossible to tell anyone the whole saga, just as it's impossible to "see" a whole city. You can see a street, cars going by, the windows of the building across the way, the trees in a park, but no one can see the city.

Little by little they stopped asking me about him, or else they would say quietly, with a very serious expression, "How's your son?"

They were surprised when I, in turn, would ask, "Which of my sons?" They seemed to have forgotten about the others' existence. But what did my answer matter? I would get that dull pain that isn't quite a pain in the pit of my stomach and answer as best I could, but I was always dissatisfied; I felt judged and condemned for being a bad mother. I asked myself for the umpteenth time: "Why did all this happen? Why couldn't I have prevented it?"

A mortal lethargy filled me every time I left the luxurious neighborhood where my office was located, La Recoleta, a bit of Paris in Buenos Aires, with its mansions, its broad expanses of green, and its refined restaurants and shops. Those weren't happy days, but they were peaceful, and peace was almost the same as happiness to me. Until my contract with the Ministry expired and wasn't renewed. They organized a pro forma search, and I applied, although I knew they'd give the job to someone else. In any event I needed to return to my normal activities.

In order to make – and abide by – the decision to stop seeing and financing Federico, I required the assistance of an army of doctors, psychologists, lawyers, social workers, all my closest friends, and a high retaining wall of pink pills. But I managed to do it. Between Federico and me there existed that abnormal, sick phenomenon that specialists call symbiosis (one of them mentioned the term casually, and it's possible he later regretted it: teaching patients the technical names of their problems never helps solve them). *The sickness is in the connection*, they explained to me. I couldn't change the connection; it was necessary to sever it surgically.

I stopped seeing him three years ago. The anguish I feel when I awaken isn't so intolerable anymore. Whenever I leave the spa and go to Buenos Aires for a few days, I find some message on the answering machine. He no longer begs to see me. I found out that after he ran away, he and his new girlfriend lived in a fleabag hotel.

As soon as I disappeared from Federico's life, he improved. Expressed in technical terms, my submission and the symbiosis had exacerbated the picture. Free to fend for himself, he found a job and has kept it. Precisely because he's held onto it for two years, I have to conclude that he's stopped taking drugs. After a few months he moved from the hotel to a rented room in an old house in San Telmo and then to a small downtown apartment. When he calls me, his voice is sometimes enthusiastic, but more often he sounds ill-humored and angry to me, as if he didn't understand how he lost everything he's lost. Once he insinuated we might see each other, and I tried to remind him of the things that had happened. He said it was unbelievable that I still kept harping on "that" – "all that stuff happened three years ago." He referred only to the fact that he ran away from the Lezama Center before he was discharged, as though I had amnesia about everything that had transpired before. At last, in another conversation, I managed to tell him that "that" – the abuse – had lasted for years, and this time he didn't reply. Shortly thereafter, he called one more time and, in a dry, disagreeable tone, asked me to buy him some book so he could learn to play poker.

For one second, for one single second, I imagined myself scouring bookstores and tobacconists where they sell cigars from all over the world, imported liquor, tumblers with dice, little, personal-size roulette wheels, in search of a book of poker instructions. If I had still nursed any hope, it was now clear that I couldn't guarantee I'd ever be able to see Federico again. And not only because of what he might do but also because of what I myself might be capable of doing.

Today, on this magnificent morning by the sea in San Conrado, on the threshold of this day that's just beginning, I think that I've spent my whole life beginning. Many of them were pleasant things that I began again of my own free will, like having a child when my other children were already teenagers. Of course it didn't turn out as I'd expected, because I'd forgotten that between the original deed, which you begin for the first time, and the one you repeat in order to regain that happiness, not only happiness, but also time, passes you by. You're no longer the same, and you can't enjoy things in the same way. When Federico was born, Francisco was twenty and Tomás was fifteen. I was no longer twenty-something, and although my physical appearance hadn't changed so much, I was no longer a gloriously young mother proudly pushing a double baby carriage holding a five-month-old infant and a two-and-a-half-year-old child. Neither did I have the energy I had then, when I carried both of them in my arms, the older one sitting on my left hip, the baby in the hollow of my right arm, as if I were a fertility symbol.

Federico had several different kinds of chairs, carriages, and swings, and a bunch of people around to care for him and play with him; I had advanced at my job and was much busier, so I accepted all the help other people offered me. In the first place Berta, who, at eighty, tried to use three-year-old Federico's skateboard and fell down, fracturing a finger on her right hand. When I returned home, I found her holding her finger under a stream of cold water from the faucet. When things became complicated, I felt a combination of pain and fatigue in my stomach that I hadn't experienced before; I think it was the first sign that nothing was the same anymore.

But now, looking out the window every few minutes in order to spot Steve on the beach, I remember last night's dream. In the dream I was at home, not in a beach hotel in another country. I was looking out the window, and the first thing I saw was a crowd of people gathered around the body of a man in a dark-blue suit. It was the body of a man lying face down on a road, probably dead, with one arm beneath his body and the other extended out. No one came near him or touched him. This scene was repeated several times. I stopped looking out the window for some time (for some time, the inexpressible time of dreams), and when I went to look again, I always saw an accident victim, a man in a dark-blue suit. It all seemed to take place at another time, maybe in 1940. I had no doubt that he'd been run over by a car. In my dream I knew that the road I saw from my window wasn't simply a city street; it was a new, high-speed, dangerous thoroughfare.

I awoke all upset, sorry that Steve had already left. It was ten a.m. I never stay in bed so long, but the night before I had gotten up while Steve was still sleeping because I couldn't fall asleep. I went to the kitchen in the suite, made myself some tea with milk and toast (I believe that tea with milk and toast is a sure cure for anxiety and other ills), looked at the sea, and sat down to write some foolishness, like someone playing scales on the piano. At a different time in my life I was as nocturnal as a moth, writing by the light of a lamp against which summer insects crashed.

The dream was one of those that don't disappear or can be forgotten, and that's exactly why I would have liked to forget it. The most tragic thing about the body in the street was that it belonged to that era. The man in the blue suit, sprawled face down in the road, could have been my dead father (he died in the 1940s); he could have been Dardo's father with his custom-tailored suits, a politician, a traveling salesman, one of those lawyers who always go around in formal clothing, one of those sick exhibitionists who expose themselves to schoolgirls on the corner. A blue suit, black shoes with laces, cuff links. It could never have been Steve, with his sports clothes, his blue eyes, and his lovely, lined face – Steve, who at that moment opened the bedroom door and leaned over to give me a kiss. And I hadn't even brushed my hair. As he kissed me, I reached for the hairbrush that I deliberately leave on the night table every night, but he ruffled my hair with his hands.

"Has my darling had coffee yet?" he asked.

Poor Steve. I've nagged him so much to call me *vos* instead of *tú* and to substitute Argentine equivalents for his Mexican vocabulary, that he almost always opts for the third person, which amuses me.

"No, Steve, I just woke up." We had our arms around one another, with my head resting on his shoulder, hoping he'd loosen his embrace so I could go brush my teeth.

"The weather's not so nice anymore," he says as we sit down at the kitchen table to have coffee.

It's true. I hadn't noticed; in just a few minutes it had grown cloudy and stormy.

"Tonight the Finns put on their play," he adds.

Of course. I'd forgotten. We'll have dinner in the little spa hotel, and later we'll watch that Finnish couple put on a comedy skit. He's a theatrical director, and she's an actress.

Now that I've showered and am wrapped in a bath towel at the breakfast table, I feel much better. I smile, showing my sparkling teeth. My mouth smells like mint.

"You know, Cecilia, I'm selling my house in Los Angeles."

"Steve . . ."

We've had this conversation before. Let's not push things, I told him. Let's keep everything the same. He replied that we couldn't stay at the spa forever or in my Buenos Aires apartment, either, and in any case we were living together. Steve picks up the dishes after meals; in that respect they've domesticated him, but in every other way he still thinks and acts like a man. He sells a house, buys a house, pays the bills, chooses a woman. I looked at him a little fearfully. Just as I try to repeat past happiness, it's possible that I might also want to repeat my adventures, run the risks. Start over. At my age. I see myself in a charming little ivory suit, with a bouquet of flowers in my hand in an ecumenical wedding ceremony. Neither Steve nor I is religious, but, if I have to get married, I'd like to have something I've never had: a beautiful ceremony. But what am I saying? It doesn't matter – let's go on: a beautiful ceremony with a Third World Catholic priest (do they still exist?) and a very progressive rabbi. Fortunately, Steve comes from an Irish Catholic family. I've lived among Catholics and Jews, and I know them like the palm of my hand. On the other hand, I know nothing at all about Protestants. I'd like to feel at home on my wedding day.

"Next time we go to Buenos Aires, will we visit your family?" Steve asks in his odd Spanish, a blend of English and Mexican nuances. He doesn't know what I was thinking about.

"Does my darling believe in God?" he once asked me.

"I believe in the God of the holy images."

"What's that?" he asked.

"Didn't my darling ever see a holy image?" I asked in turn, echoing his awkwardly formal tone. "I know they still exist. Not too long ago, when I was in Naples with Tomás, who had gone there for a few days to do some research on San Gaetano, someone gave me one. Holy images are little laminated pieces of cardboard on which God frequently appears. There are also holy images of the Virgin and the saints. But God shows up in lots of them, and that's how you can tell He exists: He's in the images, in Renaissance paintings, in Bach chorales. He exists."

Steve stares at me, fascinated. He doesn't believe a word I'm saying, but he finds it amusing. I let him lean over the cups, the coffeepot, the toast, to give me a kiss.

Does He exist? How quickly I lose interest in the subject.

If I look backward, I see chaos. That chaos is my former life. I've asked many people what they see when they look backward at their own lives, and their replies astonish me: some see an orderly place where there are many people and things, it's true, but they think it would be as easy for them to choose one segment, one place from which to extract a story, as it would be for me to choose a dinner plate, a soup bowl, or a dessert dish, without even glancing at the stacks that are always lined up the same way on the shelf.

I searched in the chaos for Federico's childhood, his delicious first year of life, prepared to find the knot I couldn't untie and which surely held the secret of the drama. I always started at the beginning and quit halfway through from sheer exhaustion and the uselessness of the endeavor. It seems I was just as good and just as bad a mother as anyone else. From the age of four or five months Federico would sit in a little chair called a BabySit, secured by a safety belt like the kind they use on airplanes. The BabySit resembled certain lawn chairs, those metal frames laced with canvas strips. We put that little chair, with the baby in it, on top of a table in the middle of the patio, under an awning. It was summer, and soon it would be time to feed him lunch, which he awaited like the pigeons in the illustrations in *Billiken* magazine, four or five little chicks in the nest with their beaks open, waiting for the mother bird. That's how Federico waited for his pureed squash mixed with ground beef, his soup, his applesauce. He began eating solid foods very early; it was the pediatric style of the day. At forty days the first teaspoonfuls of yogurt or orange juice strained through cheesecloth. At two months he was already eating half a container of yogurt, and I boasted about it proudly. Yes, I was proud that my baby ate yogurt.

Rosario helped me prepare meals. Like most of the women who "clean by the hour," Rosario lived outside the city. She traveled more than two hours every day to the capital. Like all these "cleaning ladies," she was a trustworthy person, and there was good reason for her to look for work so far from home: pay is better in the city.

She was twice as tall and twice as wide as me, a bit pompous; she thought she deserved to work in a more orderly house than mine. She arrived at eight a.m. on the dot, three times a week. A reliable domestic who asked me every morning, "Shall I make up the master bedroom now, *señora*?"

It made me laugh to hear her call the room Dardo and I occupied the "master bedroom," but she was right, because that's where the double bed was in which, as in all marriages, the most profound, secret, and conflictive aspects of our life in common were mastered. Strangely, Federico came into our lives five years after we started living together, when it was no longer a romance. Dardo and I fought a lot, but we still maintained an intense intimacy and great passions in common: films, used bookstores, music, dinners at Chinese restaurants. In those days ours was a complicated family, full of joy and affection. We lived with my sons Francisco and Tomás, already in the throes of adolescence, who adored Dardo. They played chess and chatted with him; Dardo addressed those questions of theirs to which neither Daniel nor I had the answers. I've always said that Francisco and Tomás had two dads, Daniel and Dardo.

Federico's arrival thrilled Tomás. He enjoyed having a little brother. He took him to the amusement park, bought him ice cream, and cared for him like a father; Francisco, on the other hand, barely a year older than Tomás, was, like many teenagers, fascinated by the world of ideas he'd just entered: the ideas lodged in his head and developed furiously, with a certain dose of fanaticism, leaving him little time to play. I'm weeping. I weep easily whenever I'm alone. I also wept during my marital spats, a strategy for getting my own way, I suppose. It never worked for me – not with Daniel, not with Dardo. Not with anyone, really. I think I must not be an effective weeper.

My second marriage was longer than the first. Twenty years, when you think back on them, are just a puff of air, and yet they were life, life in slow motion, like a sheet torn into shreds and dragged by someone down an interminable corridor. I shouldn't have said "someone," when I know full well that the one dragging the sheet can only be the fat nurse who stumbles along, balancing herself like a ship, before dawn, down the corridors of all the hospitals in the world, pushing the little cart with the thermometer, the bandages, and the blood pressure machine.

When I turn my head to look at the chaos of the past, sometimes I see only an enormous valley filled with pieces of scrap metal and trash, among which it's hard to discern anything at all. I should never let myself be tormented by the thought that I have nothing more to say; like a scavenger, I can always find something interesting amid the scraps, but that valley evaporates into the air as do all delusions of the insane when the chemical straitjacket is applied. In my calmer moments the garbage dump is transformed into fields planted with flowers and little houses with slanted roofs or even some medieval castle, and my kids are there. Or else they become golden beaches with taut muscles and mouths eagerly open for a kiss or streets where I walk like any reasonable person, going about my business and my daily errands.

In the master bedroom of the house where we lived when Federico was a baby, the bond between Dardo and me was affirmed. Was affirmed. What words human science has set into motion! I mean that Dardo and I desired one another again, and we delighted in one another; in that bedroom we said the most tender, the most piercing, and the bitterest things to one another. It was there that one body entered another body (Daddy loved Mommy so much that he went inside her body; you'll do the same thing when you're older). Daddy went inside Mommy's body long before you were born, not just nine months before in order to plant the seed. But young people don't like to hear about this; they don't like to think that the old folks also once made love. And still do.

In his BabySit Federico waves his arms and legs, with his mouth open like a pigeon. In the BabySit the child reclines at a forty-five-degree angle. Federico is still too small to sit up straight in a chair. He opens his mouth and dispatches his food, and he grows impatient between one bite and the next. On the table sit empty dishes, amid toys, books, a camera, today's paper, some tools Dardo used this morning to fix a faucet before he left for work. He didn't actually fix it: it still drips. He tried because I always tell him, jokingly, "But, Dardo, you're an engineer, and you can't fix a faucet?" The patio is made of old, yellowish tiles, some of them cracked, their corners broken off. There's one solitary plant against the dividing wall, a fern in a pot, which we inherited from the previous occupants. Federico is big for five months; he eats everything and still has his mouth open, waving his arms and legs. Rosario, who's been watching from the kitchen door, comes over with the bottle. Up, up, Federico. I'm sitting with Federico in my lap, in a chair with a broken back; it's missing a wooden slat. (Dardo, you're an engineer, and you can't fix a chair?)

After lunch Rosario brings a bottle with eight ounces of milk with cereal and sugar. Could we be overfeeding this child? But Federico can fall asleep only with the bottle, and we want him to have a nice nap. Now he's in my arms, emptying the bottle. I kiss his round cheek while he produces some incredible noises; it's his sucking style. By the time there's not a single drop left, he's sound asleep.

In this house all the rooms face the patio, and its doors have blinds that are painted dark green. I walk slowly, my gaze fixed on Federico's little face as he sleeps in my arms. I deposit him in his crib and cover him with a blanket. I stand there staring at him for a few moments.

Rosario has moved everything that was on the big table to the little wicker patio table so that she can lay the place settings for lunch. Dardo will join us for lunch. I'm in slippers, in a slightly faded summer dress. I go to the bathroom to take a shower and put on something nicer. The shower clears my head a little. From the bathroom I can enter our bedroom directly. The children, on the other hand, must cross the patio, but what does that small inconvenience matter to two teenagers who go camping in Patagonia in the summertime? The patio canopy is green; that is, it *was* green. Now it's faded and somewhat shabby.

Two p.m. We've already eaten lunch. Dardo has gone out again; Federico is asleep; the older boys are in school. I have to run an errand before the banks close, and I also need to pick up something at the drugstore. Rosario will stay home and watch the baby. When I return, Rosario "will retire" (she always talks that way: "I'm going to clean the master bedroom, *señora*; I'll retire now, *señora*"). If Federico is still sleeping when she "retires," I'll lock myself in the bathroom and scream. This habit of solitary screaming is an old one. I let out screams that sound awful, especially to a musical person like me, and they leave an ugly rawness in my throat. In this case they're my protest against a serene, orderly life. But what can a mother do? She has no choice but to be, or pretend to be, a serene, orderly person.As I walk to the drugstore, I see myself locked in a cell, without doors or windows, dirty walls, like in some public restrooms. Concrete floor. How did I end up here? My brain works swiftly. Some infernal organization has captured me and locked me up forever. I'll die in here, screaming, with no one to hear me, scraping plaster and shit to eat until I lose my mind altogether. In the cell I'll recall, as I do now, disconnected, meaningless pieces of my life: I'll see myself wandering down a street in my neighborhood; I'll see my blood in a test tube, ready to be analyzed; the word *Papa* written in chalk on piece of black slate; a gray bucket of dirty water with a rag soaking in it; a photo of my mother by the sea in 1929, among the waves, with her rubber bathing cap pulled down to her eyebrows and holding on to a rope with both hands; the furtive scurrying of rats in the attic of an old house where I once lived; beautiful gardens surrounded by an invisible electrified fence whose sparks can be detected only by dogs. I will see the planet Earth suspended in space, space suspended in Nothingness; I will have one final thought about homegrown tomatoes, which you can't find anymore, and I will fall silent. I'm at the intersection of two avenues, clutching a paper from the bank in my hand as if it were a passport to normalcy. I have two teenage children and a baby; I must cross the street carefully and go home.

Sometimes I'd really love to be a North American woman, one of those who star in a TV series or in the movies! Always in sports clothes, about to go jogging or running toward the sun, a woman

95

who knows exactly who she is and what she is and who knows the laws of her country by heart and who has a wardrobe filled with brightly colored clothing, not all black, brown, and gray like the ones we Argentines wear. If those women ever get sick with cancer, if they have to sleep in shelters whenever it snows relentlessly in New York, if they aren't sure if they've been good mothers, regardless of whether they're white, black, Polish, South African, Chinese, Japanese, Mexican, no matter – they can still proudly wear their uniform of T-shirts and jeans and cry discreetly at the end of a trial in which they've been declared innocent or guilty. Those women never seem to wonder where we're going or where we've come from.

I wonder what would happen if I called him up right now and said, "Federico, son, how are you?" Would he feel like running to embrace me, too? Or would he just think of it as an opportunity to ask me for something? What did I do wrong? Didn't I love him enough? How much is enough?

How much time will it take for him to remember what he's forgotten and for me to begin to forget, if, in fact, that can ever happen? Could this back-and-forth between remembering and forgetting be part of the symbiosis, as if we two were a single, inflated balloon that bulges on one side if it's squeezed on the other?

Maybe I should have stayed longer at Federico's bedside at night. My job is to invent stories, but I could never invent one for him.

I'm so afraid of night
'Cause I'm too romantic

sings Bing Crosby in the near darkness of the little, 1940s-style café on the twentieth floor of the hang gliders' building. Steve and I still have dinner in the revolving restaurant, and afterward we have a drink and dance to slow music in the tiny bar. The other customers, the pale Finns, observe us, no doubt realizing that Steve and I, who at first each went our own way and hardly even greeted each other, now share a table in the dining room and sleep in the same room. I doubt it matters much to them, and I don't think they talk about us. They're almost all men, and they all look alike. But among them there's a couple, the theatrical director and the actress, with a six-year-old adopted daughter. We chat with them from time to time. They never told us what brought them to the spa. We know that the girl is adopted because they told us so, and it's obvious: she's a small, indigenous Bolivian child, dark-skinned, with straight, shiny black hair and slightly slanted eyes. They adopted her when she was four, in Bolivia. She was living on the street and had cigarette burn marks on her body. Once I saw her in the arms of her Scandinavian mother, sobbing convulsively as children do when they've been crying for a while, if they've had a long tantrum and no one has responded to their screams. I admired the impassive Finn, who did what one should do about kids' unwarranted tantrums: ignore them. That child was really her daughter, I thought. It doesn't matter that she was four years old when she adopted her or that they found her on some Bolivian street. The fact that the child had suffered hunger and abuse didn't make the mother relent. She knew she had to train her, form her character.

That night, after dinner at the hotel, the woman recited a monologue from a play in Finnish, and Steve and I stayed to see her. Despite the fact that they told us the plot in English beforehand, we couldn't understand a thing, only that it was supposed to be funny, because the Finns laughed, decorously covering their mouths with their hands. Later we had a drink with them.

"Is it really very cold in Finland?" Steve asked.

"No, no," the couple answered in unison.

What does "very cold" mean to a Finn?

In a 1911 issue of *Caras y Caretas* magazine, there's an advertisement for a nerve tonic. "THE DANGERS OF DESPAIR," it says at the top of the page, and there's a picture of a young woman resting one arm on the table with her forehead on her arm. If she drinks the restorative tonic the drawing represents, which comes in a squat brown bottle with a diagonally placed label that reads "IPERBIOTINA MALESCI," she'll be able to laugh and sing and swing in the garden again, drink a hesperidin and soda, and feel that all her organs are in their rightful places inside her body.

I woke up suddenly, and the first thing I saw was that advertisement in *Caras y Caretas* on the floor, next to the bed. I tried to arrange my pillows: one fell on top of the alarm clock and the glass of water on the night table. When I was fully awake, I found, next to *Caras y Caretas*, *The Ballad of the Sad Café* in a Bantam edition with white covers, all soaked and wrinkled.

I leaped out of bed and ran barefoot to the kitchen to make coffee. After I drank it, my head began to function with a slight buzz, and I felt a wave of life returning.

It's Sunday. The neighbors who went to the country have kindly left the street empty for me. *The Ballad of the Sad Café*, now drying in the sun on the balcony, accompanied me when Dardo and I went to El Tigre. I read it in the afternoons, on the verandah at the back of the house, while Tomás and Francisco sailed up and down the creek in a rubber boat, ducking their heads whenever the water level rose beneath the tree branches.

A solitary afternoon at home in Buenos Aires. I discovered some old manuscripts that had been saved in a light-blue cardboard folder.

"Old? How old are those manuscripts, sweetie?" asks the Caribbean voice of dubbed North American movies.

"From 1983," I reply.

"What were you doing in 1983, sweetie?"

99

"I was at a university in Illinois with thirty other writers from different countries."

The Caribbean voice clicks off. And my invisible conversation partner disappears.

Among the papers of that period I also find a very sad letter from Dardo. How painful it is to recognize his nice, even, elegant hand on some yellow sheets written on both sides. Both of us had agreed that I should accept the fellowship; Federico, who was ten years old at the time, would be fine with his father and grandmother in Buenos Aires. I would telephone every week, and later he would come up and meet me and his brothers in Paris, and we would spend a few weeks together. It all seemed sensible when we planned it, but Dardo and I argued a lot about money, and we kept spending whatever there was with no thought of the future. I could count on three or four months of peace thanks to the fellowship, but when Dardo exhausted our resources buying film encyclopedias and whole sets of LP's, he found himself in trouble and insistently begged me to return. It was also hard for him to handle Federico by himself. I refused to interrupt my stay. If I had returned to Buenos Aires at that moment, maybe things would have improved. I thought about my career and my life. I was fifty years old. Had my life already become a one-way trip?

My arrival in Chicago was like a kid's visit to Disneyland. For as long as I could remember, I had dreamed the great North American fantasy, a conglomeration of movie stars, Crosby and Sinatra songs that I adored at age twelve, revered presidential figures who always told the truth, charming Negroes with their jazz and enormous smiles, and a little farther in the background, angry Negroes from Harlem, barely distinguishable, a dark photograph of the Vietnam War, dead soldiers in the mud and rain, a mansion seen from outside, as I've seen them for almost my entire life in every part of the world, a little kitchen in Manhattan where a drunk spends his days in filth and squalor. Sharpshooters firing at a crowd. Children who suffer sexual abuse and the trials where those abuses are dealt with. A man trembling like a leaf, strapped to the gurney on which he will be executed by lethal injection. And Christmas, *la Navidad*, you can open your presents now, sweetie, says the Caribbean voice that's returned. Just rip it open, and you'll find what you asked Santa for.

There were two Spanish speakers in the strange group in Chicago: the writer from Mexico and the one from Spain. The Mexican, Tomás Segovia, wrote lovely erotic sonnets. The writer from Spain was a communist, and he'd been in jail in Carabanchel. He was an atheist who got annoyed when he discovered that his mother had sewn a miraculous medal in the lining of his pocket. Oh, if only I'd had a mother like that! This Spaniard didn't know a word of English, and he spent countless hours contemplating the routes to other places. His dream was to go to California. At some of our gatherings, very late at night, when the entire campus slept and only the boozy writers who represented the world were still awake, singing songs of their countries, he sang the songs of the Spanish Civil War, and he sang the Internationale while thrusting his fist into the air, and those of us who could joined in.

The Bulgarian, when he dressed formally, wore the embroidered, white peasant shirts of his country. He was the master of the countryside, the one who pointed out natural beauty, the river, the elegance of a domed house. We all lived in a student dormitory, in pairs of connected rooms, with bath and kitchen in between. Not only did the writers come from every part of the world, but none of them, at least on the surface, was what he claimed to be. The Turk wasn't just any Turk: he was the head of the Ottoman Empire. The Irishman was an Anglophile. The Romanian was the master of sophistication; the Egyptian, the master of intelligence; the southern Indian, the master of shrewdness and, at the same time, a very vulnerable man who was constantly offended by the others' reactions. These reactions were naturally a product of cultural differences, like the time he was angry all night long because he entered the Irishman's room without knocking and had the door slammed in his face; surely in India people enter others' rooms without knocking. The Norwegian woman, my suite mate, was the queen of youth: she was barely twenty-six and had a fellowship from her munificent country so she would lack for nothing. The black South African, who had lost a daughter to drug addicts on a street in Johannesburg, was the queen of the victims of discrimination. The writer from Ghana, a man with brilliant black skin, was president of a university and was the master of savoir faire and diplomacy. The West German woman was the mistress of strength: she could put away astonishing quantities of alcohol from six p.m. until dawn, and we would carry her to bed, practically unconscious; the next morning, without even eating breakfast, she would write for six hours and then, before starting to drink, she would walk through the streets of the city. The Brazilian was the mistress of Latin American feminism; the East German, a blond, tall, muscular man with a baby face, was the master of affability.

I don't know what they thought of me, how they categorized me. I drank much more than usual, although not as much as the rest. At the conclusion of all the cultural gatherings, the receptions with local writers, the roundtables where identity was invariably discussed, came trays of scotch, bourbon, beer, vodka, and an unimaginable variety of peanuts, one more delicious than the next, and raw vegetables that I had always eaten cooked – leeks, cauliflower, green onions – which you were supposed to dip in spiced cream cheese before you bit into them. When, after my stay in Illinois, I walked into my hotel room in San Francisco, where I was to stay for a few days, I discovered something that left me speechless, something I didn't have in my extremely humble room at the university: a full-length mirror. There I saw a woman I hardly recognized, with an enormous belly and rolls of fat around her hips.

This was the visible result of my eternal tendency to imitate others: when I'm invited to dance, I dance; when I'm invited to drink, I drink. I staggered among the wonderful smells and tastes of the food and drink of the world that we bestowed on one another, unconsciously navigating through that experiment, the dangerous children's game that the program afforded us as proof that writers – a different sort of human species, according to them, and not recognized as such – were capable of living together even though they might be from the opposite ends of the earth. And, of course, it was true: how could we wage war on each other if we were so drunk we could hardly move?

Three months is a long, long time to be far from home. A month and a half after I arrived in Illinois, I received Dardo's letter. I didn't calmly refuse to return but, rather, was tortured by a sense of duty that condemned me to stay away from Dardo and Federico for a few more weeks. In any event canceling the fellowship was something that simply wasn't done, except in the case of serious problems; all the fellows, who endured that test of resistance to human heterogeneity with greater or lesser tolerance, would have found it absurd even to think of returning to their countries ahead of time.

When I got back to Buenos Aires, I tried to convince Dardo not to go through with the separation. It was useless, so we spent a year apart, I in a couple of rooms rented to me by a friend, and he in an apartment in Caballito, with Federico. Our moves became more frequent, sometimes with only a few months in between. Every day I picked up Federico at school and clumsily tried to restore to him what I had supposedly taken away during my three months' absence.

In truth Dardo and I never were able to separate completely. We went out together. I spent every night at his apartment until Federico fell asleep. Little by little, I distanced myself mentally from the human panoply of the international writers' meeting. The face of the Hungarian woman, who was also a doctor, faded from my memory, as did that of Reuel Molina Águila, the Filipino writer who didn't know a word of Spanish, only English and Tagalog, the native language he had been forbidden to speak in school as a child. I forgot the face of the Nigerian poet Amos Totuola. Totuola was a tribal chief in his country; he arrived in Chicago dressed and bejeweled like a character from the *Thousand and One Nights*, and a few weeks later, in jeans and a T-shirt and short hair, he had to tell me who he was so that I could recognize him; and I forgot Marianne, the Norwegian who, during her stay, received three letters informing her that friends had committed suicide. What's wrong with them?

she asked herself. Can't they bear it? She was referring to life; she thought her friends couldn't bear living.

During the final days, when I could no longer tolerate being part of that group of humanity in which I couldn't find anyone who resembled me and couldn't say so because they would have accused me of discrimination, I began to think: "Living with the whole world at the same time is hell."

When summer arrived at the end of that year, I knew Dardo was planning a vacation at the beach with Federico and Sebastián. It seemed like a good idea to me theoretically, but that night, which by chance we didn't spend together, when Federico went to sleep, I returned to the rented rooms where I was living. I thought about Dardo at the beach with the boys, by that sea I loved so much and which had received me year after year, every summer for as long as I could remember, and my anguish was so great that I phoned Dardo to ask him to meet me. We talked for hours in an old café on Avenida Corrientes, and at the end of our conversation we agreed that after New Year's, we would go to the seashore with the boys and then I'd go back and live with him.

At the end of the conversation neither one of us was euphoric; as we spoke, I thought, "He has much less hair." "He's a little more stooped than he used to be." "There's a tightness at the corners of his mouth that I never noticed before."

I never could stay away from home for too long. I'm proving that now, in the rainforest: I need to return to Buenos Aires in order to prove that my place still exists. I might have left the spa forever if I hadn't met Steve. This afternoon we took my usual walk together, the one I'd taken by myself until now, and we gathered bunches of wildflowers. Steve's bouquet was lush, compact, organized. Not mine. The flowers stems were of varying lengths, and there were too many leaves. We arrived at my waterfall; Steve had a flask of vodka in his pocket. We drank and fell asleep on a bed of leaves. I dreamed I was flying, spinning in circles like a moth around a light. When we awoke, we took a dip in the waterfall, returned to the hotel, plopped onto the bed, and Steve fell asleep before I did. I looked at his tired, lean face. He didn't have that aura of eternal youth that he reflects when he launches himself into space on his hang glider, and it occurred to me that his loneliness must be greater than mine. He doesn't even tell anyone his story, while I, by writing it, tell mine ad nauseam. Poor Steve! Poor biologist! Poor architects, plumbers, economists, entrepreneurs, surgeons, highway workers, mail carriers, telephone operators, poor lawyers, bricklayers, civil servants, math professors, concierges, deputies and senators, beggars and bums, newspaper hawkers and chamberlains, who have no opportunity to tell their fear and sadness! It's no surprise that almost all of them keep hidden away, in some drawer that only they know about, a few written pages, openly confessional or slightly disguised, that they've never shown anyone else.

I've been telling my story for no less than forty years. My books are like those travel guidebooks that show diagrams of ancient ruins, with transparent sheets of ink drawings that flip over the diagrams to illustrate what the houses and temples might have once looked like.

I've just looked at the inside of my wrists, that very delicate area between the arm and the hand where you can see very clearly the veins that must be cut, after immersing yourself in a bathtub filled with warm water, in order to extinguish life. I've never given it serious thought, but on more than one occasion I've been able to understand suicides, and it was a dangerous kind of understanding.

I rest my arm on Steve's forehead, but he doesn't move. I fall asleep.

The directors of the spa invited the whole group to a meeting, that is, us and the pale Finns. We communicated in English, but the dialogue was very similar to the one the parents at the Lezama Center had. We could only half-comprehend what was happening to us, and we found ourselves in something like a state of stupefaction. Many of us drowned our anxiety alone in whiskey or vodka; at the meeting we tried to drown it in words. We spoke for hours. Each of us saw our lives like something on a screen: we saw our country, our language, our skin. Many complained of vague illnesses, saying that when they were alone they vomited, cried, felt afraid. I looked at Steve's taut face. He was suffering, too. I was ashamed that all that time he had been looking after me as though I were the only sufferer, catering to my artist's fancies.

That night, wide awake beside Steve, who slept with a softer, relieved expression, I once more recalled my brief exile in Illinois, and in particular the Israeli writer, whom an accident had left mutilated. "A farm accident," he said without further details. Had a tractor run him over? What would our faces look like if they truly revealed life's accidents? The writer from Ghana wept because he couldn't return to his country for the birth of his child; the Irishman, who stank of dark beer, was always searching for a North American heiress who would marry him so that he could remain in the United States.

I turn on the TV and put on my earphones so I won't wake Steve. On one of the cable channels there's a show where they're discussing sexual problems and accidents. If a girl is sexually assaulted by her father, a panelist says, above all she should *communicate it* to someone (that's what I've always said, how important it is to talk, to relate). She should seek help. If no psychologist is available, she should look to her family, her community, or her congregation, for someone with greater authority or something like that. Herpes. If someone is suffering from genital herpes, he should tell his partner in a loud voice, "I have herpes." Group sex? It's fairly uncommon in the United States, but it definitely exists. Masturbation is a normal, legitimate practice. I turn off the TV and fall asleep again; it will still be here tomorrow: my married life with Steve, even though we haven't had the religious ceremony, our brief trips, my work.

I've become more interested in what Steve does; he doesn't say anything, but his smiling face, less tense, reveals that he's happier. In the afternoon he always works for a few hours in his tidy room, which he's arranged in a most pleasant way. When he tires of his biology tomes, he plays the flute; then, prodded by me, he tries to read some poem by Fernando Pessoa, from a book I brought along to the rainforest. Poems don't interest him. But I can no longer deny that what I feared has happened: once again I have a man by my side who needs me and whom I need. *I'm* no longer at the rainforest spa: *we*, Steve and I, are at the rainforest spa.

What remnant of the day made me dream about a shark in the bathtub? How easy it would be to interpret the dream, without the interpretation's being less valid than many other interpretations. Could the shark represent time, devouring my existence? The shark in my dream was perfectly tame. The bathtub was a little smaller than normal; it must have been three feet long, and the shark was approximately the same size. Precision doesn't matter in dreams. I didn't know what he ate, but he seemed like a healthy, strong shark, and maybe the cleaning woman took care of feeding him, just as she takes care of watering the plants on the balcony. I didn't feel it was dangerous to keep him in the house, despite the shape of his mouth and the number of teeth he had, which I didn't have a chance to count because I didn't see him with his mouth open. I felt more or less safe because I realized that the shark couldn't get out of the bathtub, and especially because he was wide awake, so he wouldn't be startled by a sudden noise: everyone knows that a startled animal can bite. But this was a tame shark, perhaps a baby shark. Recalling the dream as I heated water for tea in the kitchen, I thought that if the shark developed his instincts, he might play a dirty trick on us.

When we're in Buenos Aires, Steve uncomplainingly accepts my orders to spend entire days without seeing me or phoning me, so that I can devote myself to work. That is: so I can apply the terrible, controversial technique of inducing suffering in order to be able to talk about it, just as actors induce it in order to act. Didn't Pasolini ask his own mother, who played the role of the Virgin Mary in *The Passion According to Saint Matthew*, to remember the death of her own son in the war in order to make her anguished crying at the death of her son, Jesus Christ, seem more realistic? This induced pain artists practice is like a dream.

"His conduct leaves much to be desired," Federico's teacher had written on his report card. He was twelve when we took a few days' vacation in Entre Ríos, at the home of one of Dardo's friends. Federico amused himself annoying an enormous, very ugly dog, just to frighten me; he enjoyed scaring me. The house was very pretty, as was the countryside; the sun set behind a hill of eucalyptus, and I invented the ritual of having all of us sit on the verandah to watch the sun set behind the tree trunks. I put on a Paco de Lucía recording, and we watched twilight descend accompanied by his guitar. All of us, even Federico, participated in the ceremony.

The dog was a repulsive mixture of bulldog with some other, unknown breed, or several. He had a huge snout and terrifying fangs. He spent his life tied up, because if they had let him loose in the country, he would have killed calves and lambs. It was no treat for me to wake up to the sweet fragrance of the flowers and the cackling of the hens and sit down to breakfast on the verandah with that great, drooling maw in plain sight. Federico went over to torment him, and in spite of the fact that the dog was tied up, I began to scream. Then Federico grew bolder and poked a stick at his eyes. One more badly begun day, one more day when I would be forced to leave the house with Federico and Sebastián, who was a serious, studious boy, to walk a mile down the boring path to town so that the kids could play pinball games in a ramshackle grocery, far from the dog.

It was a road untraveled by a single soul, only us, trudging beneath a searing sun, among thistles and wasteland, until, on one of those outings, we saw a broken-down vehicle approaching, inside which there seemed to be no one but a peasant with a torn undershirt and a fierce expression. I did feel fear – nearly paralyzing fear – when the vehicle stopped. It looked like one of those buses that are abandoned in scrap heaps in Buenos Aires, ruined, with no glass in the windows, dented, and with flaking paint and rust eating into the metal all over, although you could tell that it had once been painted yellow. The man asked me a question. It was an innocent question.

"You know where the Vélez farm is?"

The boys stopped a little behind me.

"That way, that way," I replied, pointing to the road we had come from, although I had never heard of the Vélez farm.

"We been there already; it ain't there," the man answered.

Then I saw them. I looked inside the bus and saw a pile of men resembling the driver, asleep, or rather sprawled on the floor of the vehicle, all jumbled together like cattle. They were all barefoot; they wore only tattered pants and holey undershirts, and just a few of them were asleep or almost asleep, most likely sleeping off the last of a hangover. One or the other, with great effort, raised his head to look at me and stared me up and down, the way a man eyes a woman. I was much younger than I am now, and men still looked at me like that. At some point in my life, I stopped getting those stares, and I understood that time had passed, that damned time you notice only when it's passed. Whoever sees a plant grow? Who sees a sunbeam disappear from a room, that sunbeam that at first was next to the door, then playing against a mirror and suddenly on the back wall? I didn't notice exactly at what moment men's gazes, calculating and anxious, which used to run up and down my body, were replaced by calm looks, directed toward my eyes, looks that reflected a certain fondness and much – too much – respect.

I turned to the boys, who were about thirty feet behind me, holding hands. I saw that one of the men piled on the floor of the bus tried uselessly to stand up and then fell again like a sack of potatoes, but my fear didn't abate. Suddenly, the two boys ran to my side. Sebastián took my hand. With his other hand he held Federico.

"Let's go, Cecilia," he said.

I stopped looking at the bus driver and the men, many of them now awake, who stared at me and stared at the boys with half-closed, reddened eyes, and we started walking as fast as we could without running. We passed the bus, and I felt a chill down my back as we left it behind. I heard the man at the wheel shouting, but I didn't turn around; my sweaty T-shirt clung to my back, and I couldn't help thinking that the driver would suddenly turn around and follow us. I imagined a scene in which the drunks, now wide awake, would climb off the bus and attack us, robbing and raping us. How were they to know I only had five pesos in my wallet? We pressed forward frenetically – although not running – and suddenly heard the noise of an engine sluggishly turning over, making me feel as though my kidneys were being ripped out. This time I couldn't avoid turning around, and I noted with relief that the bus was continuing in the same direction, that is, away from us. At the grocery store in town I bought sausages and soap powder; the boys played pinball, and we returned by the same route. At last we reached the country house, where Dardo was calmly reading the paper on the breezy verandah. I burst out crying. Why had he let the boys and me walk into town alone? I told him the story. He looked at me, perplexed, without putting down the newspaper; he looked at the boys, who were trying to scramble between two pieces of barbed wire fence. They had already learned, just as I did when I was taken to the country at their age, to step on the lower wire with the sole of their sneakers and lift the upper one very carefully, grabbing it somewhere between two barbs. That's exactly what they did, vanishing from our sight toward the eucalyptus grove.

When it was time for me to furnish my current apartment, like so many times before, I first organized the living-dining room; I installed small bookshelves, separated from one another so that they wouldn't seem overwhelming; I placed photographs and other small, beloved objects on the shelves, the statuette of a fleshy bather about to take a plunge, purchased in Stockholm at a place called "Very Swedish," and the wooden miniature Humpty Dumpty. With what I had left, I bought more armchairs, a broad, low coffee table, and I polished the grandfather clock that's eternally stuck at five in the afternoon.

> *Ignacio climbs the steps,*
> *Bearing his death on his shoulders.*
> *At five in the afternoon.*
> *At exactly five in the afternoon.*[1]

And I see Alice, arriving at the Mad Tea Party to join the March Hare and the Mad Hatter. There, in Wonderland, they'll spend their whole lives having tea because the Queen's curse has made it eternally five in the afternoon.

An e-mail message from Steve: he's arriving tomorrow, after a quick trip to Los Angeles. His son, Donald, was temporarily released from the rehab center and is living with his mother in Claremont. I don't envy that woman.

Ezeiza. I don't find any airport attractive, but I both love and hate Ezeiza. I feel intact, strong, young, frivolous, and happy, although I keep asking myself the idiotic questions we became accustomed to in the twentieth century, with its insistence on discussing and classifying everything: what's better, good sex or tenderness and com-

---

1. Federico García Lorca, "Lament for Ignacio Sánchez Mejía."

panionship? Can sex be classified as good, bad, or indifferent? I've seen people destroyed by divorce, people who got divorced because their "sex lives were unsatisfactory." But when you separate, you separate altogether: the mediocre sex ends, true, but also the presence of the other person, the warmth of his hand, some kind words at the opportune moment, the beautiful feeling of being in a nest as a storm rages outside, and the hope of a happier life together.

As time passes and one approaches sixty, isn't it natural that the peaks of sexual pleasure should be less steep than they were in the past? It's well known that intimacy in bed can also change ideas.

The automatic doors open, releasing Steve, bearing a small valise and a large smile.

Is this happiness? I ask myself as Steve sleeps beside me. Or is happiness what the young mother feels in the *Reader's Digest* story?

Exhausted after a terrible day with the kids, Mary wipes the sweat from her forehead and lifts her face toward her husband.

"Mary, darling, is dinner ready yet?"

"Yes, yes, darling, but could I take a quick shower first? The children are already asleep. What do you think, darling?"

"Marvelous, my dear, but how about we take a shower together?"

"You're a devil, baby, but, after all, we're only young once."

That night, as they both lie in bed with the window wide open, letting in the heat and humidity, Mary reasons that Rhonda is just a six-month-old baby, so she rolls her carriage into the bedroom to let her sleep by her side. Just in case she wakes up at midnight, wanting to nurse.

"You shouldn't be nursing her in the middle of the night anymore, honey."

And Mary smiles, and when he's asleep she brings in the carriage. Rhonda, delicious, plump, and bald, lets out a little cry at midnight, and Mary picks her up, putting her to her breast, and Rhonda nurses contentedly. Mary wipes her forehead and sniffs the scents of the bed and the delicate fragrance of the baby and the perfume of flowering trees that filters in through the window with the breeze. I must find out, she thinks; first thing tomorrow I'll do the pregnancy test, and if I'm pregnant, there'll be five kids and Rhonda will have to stop nursing.

That night Rhonda didn't go back to her crib. She slept happily between Mommy and Daddy, and that was very bad. As if those were the only bad things in life.

When we leave the spa, we'll live in Claremont, outside Los Angeles, Steve said, buttering his toast. In the morning I'll chat with the Mexican gardener; in the afternoon I'll write in my study facing the garden and the swimming pool; in the evening we'll dine at a lovely restaurant, and then we'll go into Los Angeles to see a movie or take in a concert. Of course, we'll have two houses, one in Buenos Aires and the other in Los Angeles.

Sometimes I try to forget that Steve speaks of our future as if it were entirely up to him; he pays for the spa and for the hotel suite in San Conrado. I've tried to imagine how I'd manage by myself without Steve. The rent for this apartment is very high; I'd have to move to a smaller one. What if, instead of renting, I were to buy a small apartment in a less expensive neighborhood, with a bank loan?

I could go live in Wilde, for example. Very few people, except those of us who live in the capital or environs, know about this town in the southern part of Greater Buenos Aires. Wilde is near Avellaneda. Avellaneda, however, is a well-known place. "I'm from Avellaneda," means, "I'm from a small town, not like folks from Palermo Chico. I'm from a town and proud of it." Don't some people who live in San Isidro call it Saint Isidore? Pronounced that way, English style, it reminds one of tea with scones and orange marmalade. Avellaneda never had any other name; its name immediately evokes an old bridge, the foul waters of the Riachuelo, the powerful arm of a dockworker, and Perón's smile from the 1940s. It has more strength, more character, than Saint Isidore. But it's not exactly correct to call Wilde a town, either. Towns are those of my childhood, when all you could see from the train was country, country, country, a cow, more country, a windmill, more country, a little house, two or three little houses, country, a couple of trees, and suddenly you'd find yourself on a paved street where the houses were leaning up against each other with dividing walls in between, and you'd see a business called "Madrecita's Butcher Shop and Greengrocer." Now *that* was a town, surrounded by countryside! These days the towns bordering the city of Buenos Aires are neighborhoods of a single ring-shaped city that surround the capital, where you can see, if you're crazy enough to want to drive all around it, everything from huge mansions amid old groves in the northern section to the main street of a little town full of hanging street signs and neon signs and precarious houses that you glance at quickly out of the corner of your eye (poverty is hard to digest), as you travel toward a relaxing day at a house with a garden.

Wilde is pronounced *Weel-deh* in Spanish. Anyone asking for directions who happens to pronounce it like the name of the great English writer will find himself in trouble. And it's pretentious and foolish to pronounce words in another language when speaking Spanish, because it's true that we know how to say "Wilde" instead of "Weel-deh," but in how many languages can we do it? It's better to be humble and pretend that you don't even know English. You can get to Wilde by bus, because if you start out spending money on taxis or limousines, you defeat the entire purpose of going to Wilde.

Whether or not it's cheaper to live in Wilde than in Buenos Aires remains to be seen, but it's very likely that in Wilde there's one of those square little white houses for rent, with a huge humidity stain on the front wall that the coat of paint didn't manage to conceal. The blinds on the single window, like the door, are painted bright blue, the ugliest possible shade of blue. At one side is a small garden with a rosebush. To the left of the house is a barbecue place with pieces of yesterday's roast in the window, its white grease congealed, and to the right is a gloomy and equally greasy tire store. The rent can't be more than 150 pesos a month, and there are no expenses.

I'm going to live in Wilde and cut all my extra expenses: high rent, health plan payments, Portuguese and guitar lessons; I'll toss my credit cards in the trash; I'll refuse to allow Steve to pay for me at the spa. I don't know what I'll do about Steve; I can't think about Steve and my financial uncertainties at the same time. But it seems to me I'd rather go to Wilde and keep working as a writer in the square living room of the little house than move to California. Because in the little house in Wilde there's also a living-dining room. There I'll put my armchairs and coffee table and, on the opposite side (everything a little crowded together), the table and chairs. My posters, my library. Everything inside the house is just as perfectly square as the facade, and in the bathroom there's a drip that leaves a puddle from the base of the sink to the grating. In any case I'll keep the bottle of Carolina Herrera perfume on the shelf beneath the mirror.

In Wilde I'll cancel my Internet and e-mail access, and I'll get along with ordinary mail, with the post office seven blocks away. Every time I go there, I'll help a woman who's so bent over that her back nearly parallels the floor to look up a postal code in the book that's fastened to the counter with a heavy chain. Could anyone ever have *stolen* a postal code directory at this branch?

As for everything else, well, I like cheap food. What could be a better lunch than some spaghetti in Argentine-style tomato sauce? (You fry the onion first.) And for dessert a tangerine like the ones I used to eat as a child on sunny winter afternoons, sitting in the doorway of the old house.

Steve doesn't appear in any of these thoughts, which he can't even imagine. Steve is looking for a clean knife to spread *dulce de leche* on his buttered toast.

I have to consult my doctor about the pills; they might be having an adverse effect, as it says in the literature. Although it seems unbelievable today, there was a period in my life when I didn't take pills. I took aspirins, of course, or something stronger, for headaches, and I managed to accumulate about ninety brown bottles of homeopathic drops with their poetic names and their inevitable uselessness, but I didn't take these pink pills or the white capsules that subtly change my mood and, I suppose, my thought processes. Surely when they reduce the dose of my pills, my thoughts will go back to their source, to the river of normalcy. What now seems tragic to me will become trivial and even amusing. The effect of the pills is real. One day I forgot to take them, and Federico's image returned, tall and strong and filled with fury, pushing me against the wall and staring at me with his eyes ablaze.

The doctor reduced my dose, but he warned me that I'll have to wait a few days in order to see how I really feel. Steve is at a meeting in South Africa, and I no longer enjoy being alone in Buenos Aires. It's early, barely eight thirty a.m., and it's Sunday. I won't have to face the unbearable crowds that go out strolling after noon or clog the shopping malls. In those horrid places there isn't even the protection of walls: they're like immense sheds where people buy and buy or sit down to eat something in one of the areas marked off by rows of tables that form a rectangle opposite a counter, with different colored tablecloths from the ones in the rectangle next door. There people eat without talking – it's impossible to hear – while staring at enormous photographic blowups of sandwiches, hot dogs, hamburgers, and ice cream of every imaginable hue.

I'm in a café opposite the shopping mall, and I'm watching women go in and out with big bags, sometimes with children, almost always alone. There are no men.

I step out into the street and hail a taxi. It's possible the taxi driver may tell me a grisly or perverse story: the story of a man who went to get his car out of the garage one day and carelessly backed up, running over one of his three kids. Or a love story: the taxi driver is in love with a woman, but she doesn't want to marry him, and he thinks she has another lover. But it's also possible the taxi driver won't tell me anything, and when I pay him, he might magically change the ten peso bill I gave him into a two peso bill, and I won't be able to prove to him that it's a trick. At last I reach the door of my house, and the driver says "Good luck," and I tell him, "Same to you."

I'm on my feet again. In the rainforest spa again. Who would ever guess, seeing me on the beach, next to Steve, smiling at him beneath the San Conrado sun without a trace of fear, that I've spent my life on my knees? Because I *have* spent my life that way (despite my sedate, bourgeois appearance), racked with fear, with my stomach in knots until it hurts, begging someone's pardon, begging for alms, frightened, my clothes in disarray and my hair disheveled like a vagrant. And yet, according to what I was taught, it's better to give than to receive. Did you help someone today? Whom? A tree? Your friend? Your mother? How intensely I still feel within me that twelve-year-old girl, lying face down in bed during her blissful summer vacation, reading the upbeat, moralizing stories in the *Reader's Digest!* The one about the young woman who is exhausted at the end of the day after having guided her four small children through all their school and sports activities, their feedings and bowel movements. She's in shorts, sweaty, opening the oven door to see if dinner's ready yet. In one arm she holds a baby, while another child, sitting beside her on the floor, screams himself hoarse, and her husband, who's just come home from the office, kisses her on the cheek and asks, "Were you exercising, darling?"

On my last trip to Buenos Aires I had a routine mammogram. The report says, describing my breasts: "intact." That word frightens me, although it ought to reassure me. The X-ray doesn't indicate how long I'll keep them intact. They're not even very droopy, as befits a respectable woman my age. My God, it's a quarter to nine in the morning. According to *Reader's Digest*, I should live the hours remaining to me every day until nightfall without wasting a single drop of happiness, and if I have to live on my knees, I should use that position to thank God. I don't know if He exists, but if He doesn't, I wouldn't know whom or what to thank: chance? Medicine? My DNA? But aren't those all euphemisms for the word *God*? Anyway, thank you, dear God, for allowing me to keep my breasts intact.

"I know who you are," my new gynecologist told me. I had switched from my regular gynecologist to one that was in the group authorized by my health plan; that's what I paid those high monthly premiums for. She saw my name in the papers all the time; of course, she'd never read any of my books. During that initial conversation she was very pleasant and smiling, but as soon as it was time for the physical exam, the doctor changed her attitude. Her smile vanished; she stood up, looking more serious than a pervert who's about to ravish someone, and pointed her index finger at the room next door where the examination table with its stirrups awaited. From there on she gave me a series of signs without uttering a word, except for one occasion, when, thanks to my stupidity, she had to resort to spoken language to instruct me to unhook my bra and expose my breasts, although I must admit she gestured very eloquently, and anyone more alert than I would have understood. I wanted to climb up on the table from the side. With a peremptory gesture, she indicated that I had to do so from the front. Once I was lying down, with my feet in the stirrups and my head raised so that I could see her, she made gestures with her palms turned toward her (come this way, the gesture means, slide forward a little), like those kids who help you park your car for spare change. I did, and immediately she turned her palms toward me and made a motion like telling a car to stop. "Enough, enough, don't come forward anymore, that's good." Now that my position was satisfactory (no one else but she could possibly think so), she made a broad gesture that I didn't really understand, and she was obliged to speak in order to tell me to expose my breasts. And so, spread-eagled, half-naked, and wanting it all to end as quickly as possible, I endured her disturbing words.

"There's something here; there's something here. I want an ultrasound." She guided my index finger to press a spot on my lower belly. I didn't have any idea what I was touching, but it felt like a little ball. Immediately, she began pacing around the room like a hungry rat.

"I want an ultrasound," she said nervously. "I want an ultrasound."

She asked me, "Have you ever had any bleeding?"

"Never," I replied.

"Never?" she insisted.

"No, never."

As if, nervous as I am, I wouldn't have gone running like a maniac to see her if I had been bleeding. She left me there just as I was, spread-eagled on the table, with my feet resting in the stirrups, while she paced and said, "I want an ultrasound. I want an ultrasound."

Later, returning to the sign language she seemed so comfortable with, she indicated that I should get up and get dressed (I understood that part perfectly). As I dressed, she collected her instruments, murmuring, "I want an ultrasound."

I'm not terrified yet; I never get scared right away, or maybe I just go into a frozen panic that takes away all feeling. Falsely serene, I buttoned and adjusted my clothing and followed her to her office.

By the time I sat down, she was already writing something on her prescription pad and asked me for my insurance number.

"Take care of this and come back to see me," she said.

I noticed that she used glasses with very strong magnification, and her eyes were slightly sunken, and all her earlier, stupid cheerfulness had disappeared when she recognized my name. In her waiting room I had seen and leafed through two or three magazines from a big stack on a small table, some more recent than I had ever found in a doctor's office. So, that was what she read! There were truly famous people in the magazines: the king of Spain playing tennis, a rock star making noodles in her kitchen, a football player who lived in Italy, a *vedette* who had recently gotten a divorce, a newborn baby just as ugly as all newborn babies, with that unfathomable anguish a newborn can reflect in its face, in the arms of the young wife of a TV actor. Many famous people invariably have their pictures taken in bed, even though they live in magnificent homes where there are doubtless more interesting corners.

I couldn't possibly have appeared in any of those magazines.

Little by little, fear invaded my brain.

"Could this be a fibroid?" I asked tonelessly.

By way of reply I received only silence and that ugly grimace one makes by thrusting one's lower lip forward without opening one's mouth when one prefers not to reply in words and which means, "How should I know?"

She wrote down two more things on the prescription. She began to speak, and I didn't understand what she was saying. Her eyes grew wide behind the thick lenses.

"You need to have an ultrasound," she said in a louder voice.

I had already broken with my regular gynecologist, a well-known professional (ah, and famous, too!), whom I had abandoned inopportunely in order to be examined by her. I had also broken with my equally well-known and prestigious medical clinic because of some sort of conflict between my hormones and my cholesterol, and I'd especially broken with myself for not having realized that they weren't taking good care of me and for having neglected my sexual intimacy, about which she asked impertinent questions.

She handed me a padded envelope with a snip of my beloved tissue for the Pap smear, adding (now she addressed me formally – I was no longer a famous woman who appears in the newspaper but, rather, an unfortunate woman with problems): "Yes, *because of your anxiety*, I want to do this first" (referring to the ultrasound). "Do it, and bring me the results as soon as they're ready," she said without moving a muscle.

We said good-bye; I took the prescriptions and went to the office door.

"You've never had any bleeding?" she asked again.

"Never," I replied.

"I'm not coming back here," I said to myself impetuously, filled with anger and humiliation. I could have phoned Steve, who was at the spa and who would have immediately flown to Buenos Aires to be at my side in this predicament, but I didn't. I went here and there; I had the tests the doctor recommended. Incredibly, I returned to her office.

Her attitude had changed again. She seemed calm, explaining to me with cramped, incomprehensible diagrams the state of my reproductive apparatus and saying I had a little cyst on an ovary, "which I shouldn't have at my age."

"I didn't choose to have the cyst, doctor," I said.

She went on to the uterus: there was a thickening of the wall and a fibroid. Returning to her sign language, she shook her head right and left, indicating disapproval, and spat out bluntly that a uterus like mine . . . with her usual silent gesture, which this time signified: out with it! As far as a possible hysterectomy was concerned, we'd see. Her expression softened a little, and she was kind enough to tell me a story: a patient of hers who was a vegetarian and a naturist refused to have any type of test or operation or to take medication.

"And can you imagine, what a coincidence," the doctor added, as she put the finishing touch on her story, almost tenderly, "later on, I was the one who operated on her for cancer."

Why don't you go fuck yourself, I thought, but this time I said nothing.

In order to show me the place where I had to go for the biopsy, she dismissed en masse all the clinics and hospitals on my expensive insurance plan, saying that only one of the places that appeared on the list met with her approval, a place where, incidentally, she was chief of gynecology; she knew the anesthesiologist, the surgical nurse, the pathologist . . . The chosen place was in a distant part of Buenos Aires, a hospital that, in her own words, "had shitty accommodations." Although you don't need accommodations for a biopsy, I didn't like the idea that a place where they would touch my body might be shitty. I had the blood tests, the chest X-ray, and the EKG required for general anesthesia.

The EKG envelope was open. Assuming that everything was all right with my heart, I delayed looking at it until after lunch. I had told several of my women friends of my anxiety but no men. Men get more nervous about things involving the body and blood. I saw myself naked, barely covered by a hospital gown, with several tubes shoved down my throat, waking up from anesthesia, the pain in my gut, the organs where my children were produced now extirpated, the nurse who takes too long to give me a painkiller, the painkiller that doesn't take effect right away, the nurse who brings the bedpan, the fear of urinating, the fear of defecating. And a few days later, now discomfort free, smiling, just a little pull in the incision site when I stood up, a little weak, yes, but with a broad smile. You look great, girl; you did the right thing "getting rid of all that." I saw the look of satisfaction on my doctor's face (I have to ask her if the vegetarian is still alive or if she died). It would take me a month to get over my depression, but the worry would be gone forever. What does "forever" mean? Mightn't I have cancer in some other part of my body?

Dardo, I thought. First Dardo and then, sooner or later, me.

The result of the EKG said: EKG compatible with hypertrophy (then a word I couldn't make out: *concentric* or *concentrated*) of the L.V. All else N/P."

All else no problem. So, the hypertrophy of the left ventricle was a problem. I was full of danger zones. I had a heart problem, too. I didn't feel anything. Once again the paralyzing terror. This time I did call Steve, and while he was on his way to Buenos Aires, I spoke to my dear, regular physician. "Perfect," he said. "That's the heart of someone with hypertension. You had hypertension, but you don't anymore because you're being treated for it, but while you had it, without treatment, your heart was working as if you had sent it to the gym, and the heart is a muscle. If you go to the gym to develop your biceps, when you stop going, your biceps remain developed. It would be more worrisome if you had *enlargement*, but *hypertrophy* . . ." I stopped listening because I had been transfixed by the perfectly blue sky I saw through the window. End of summer, promise of beautiful, serene autumn days, with a certain delicious melancholy at dusk.

The prospect of a biopsy in a hospital in a remote part of Buenos Aires that had shitty accommodations and the suffering and slow recovery from a hysterectomy lost their importance. My heart was all right! Because you can live without a uterus but not without a heart. At that moment I felt the relief of my trusted, old doctor's conviction.

By my tree
I lived happily . . .

125

said Georges Brassens. Of course. I should never have left my tree. I should always have returned to it. My clinic-tree. My gynecologist-tree.

Steve arrived in Buenos Aires. He's not a doctor, he's a biologist, but he agreed with me about one thing: why had I changed doctors? All around the world people know that changing a good, prestigious doctor for one of lower status (who, besides, knows the first one and had him as a professor when she was a student) is just asking for trouble. I requested an appointment and went to see my gynecologist accompanied by Steve, who busied himself leafing distractedly through a magazine while we waited. I imagined the other doctor chasing me down the street, brandishing a scalpel, all the way to the enemy clinic.

Ten days of hormone treatment got rid of the cyst and reduced the thickness of the uterine wall. The fibroid isn't significant. I know I'm all right and don't have to be rushed off to an operating room. Besides, I think having Steve in Buenos Aires is my best medicine.

At the spa: walking all day through the rainforest, stopping to rest whenever I want, returning to the hotel at dusk. Dinners with Steve, dancing in the bar at the beach. Half a pink pill and one white capsule every morning. Or half a capsule. The pink pills, the psychiatrists finally said, take them according to your level of anxiety.

Can one go back in time? I'd like to think so, to think I could sit at my portable Olivetti-Underwood again, cleaning out its grime-filled *o* with the point of a pin. I used to insert carbon paper to make several copies, as evidenced by the old papers with blue type that I look at every so often. What did I need so many carbon copies for?

My story, my memories, are repeated as if I were writing with that carbon paper again.

I'm at home in Buenos Aires, alone, together with the inevitable torment of my physical and other ailments, all old, all familiar, that assault me and get worse whenever I sit down to write but which can only be alleviated by writing. It's a sunny Sunday that reminds me of Steve and San Conrado, but here I am: alone, in pain, my head only occasionally clear, a cold sore in full bloom beneath my lower lip, covered with a gel that I involuntarily touch with my tongue ever few minutes; here I am, constantly correcting my posture (I tend to slump) and my story, always unlikely, always inconclusive, getting up every few minutes to make tea, to make coffee, to watch a portion of a TV movie.

Why do I keep taking my tranquilizer at seven in the evening and eleven at night? It's not a sleeping pill, just a tranquilizer with a bit of antidepressant in it, but I know that if I take it later in the day, I'll sleep better. I wake up early, like a schoolgirl or a manual laborer or an old woman. Everyone knows that old folks get up early in order to make noise and disturb the young, but whom do I disturb? Couldn't Steve have been confused? Could it be true he likes me just as I am, with my tragedies intact, my sense of humor, without losing ten pounds or buying myself new clothes, without toning down my irony, without ever being able to remember if he uses cream or sugar in his coffee or what time he wakes up in the morning?

I want to write, and the tears won't let me;
I try to cry, and cannot find comfort

I pick up my pen, and the tears return
All conspires against me, everything ails me.[2]

How would Lope cry? Silently, with his elbows resting on the table, covering his face with his hands. I cry out loud, like a child, screaming with my mouth wide open till I feel like the corners of my mouth could rip apart. At first the sobbing is in my stomach, and I try to calm it with boiled rice, but my stomach swells up even more, and I go out, buy a few little things, look around me at the deserted street, the service station on the corner, the multicolored fruit stand diagonally across the street, and the tears flow; I'm about to surrender to the tears right there in the middle of the street, when I see someone coming out of his house and I force myself to calm down.

If it's true Federico doesn't remember what happened, he must conclude that I'm crazy; I'm a crazy woman who makes things up in order to avoid seeing her son.

"What I did was because of the drugs."
"Yes, but you did it. And you did it to me."
"And you still remember, after so long?"
"I remember everything perfectly. Do you want me to remind you?"

Last night I dreamed of Federico again. I was giving him something. Something I clutched in my hand. In my dream I didn't know what it was. I woke up right away; the blankets were suffocating me. I had to sit up in bed, turn on the night-light. I fell asleep and dreamed again. And the same thing happened. The last time the dream was repeated, I dreamed I had a list in my hand, the list of things I was supposed to give him. We argued. In the end I didn't give him anything because once again my dream was interrupted. I turned on the light and glanced at the time: it was 6:20 a.m. It took me a few seconds to fully awaken and reassure myself that it had been a dream, that the only reality was this tragic love I can demonstrate

2. Lope de Vega, "Sonnet LII."

128

only by adhering to an iron law: not to see him, not to give him anything. Not to see him.

Once out of bed I feel better; I put on my bathrobe, walk around the house turning on lights; I heat water for coffee, collect the newspapers. Tomorrow we'll have another Monday off, a long weekend for the benefit of tourism. I return to the unmade bed, feel a little cold, cover myself with the blankets, curl up like a child.

If I dragged through this world
My shame at having been
And my pain at no longer being

Beneath the brim of my hat . . .

The melody has the same boozy melancholy as the words. Having been what? No longer being what? It seems like the singer is dragging his shame and his pain beneath the brim of his hat, but that's not what he means. "Beneath the brim of my hat" is the start of a new stanza and a new musical phrase, and I'll bet my boots that a tear is about to fall. I can see the drunk's skinny, gray face; his eyes are in shadow because his hat is tilted; the tear, enormous as a loop of dining room spiderweb, in its trajectory from his eye to the grubby table in the bar.

Cabo Polonio

I have breakfast with Steve on the beach called La Paloma, in Uruguay. I chose this spacious, clean, unpretentious hotel, and the breakfast is as unpretentious as the rooms, almost monastic but with good beds and a good shower. The coffee is excellent, and on the table there's a breadbasket overflowing with croissants (on a scale of one to ten I'd rate them five), somewhat hard toast, and buttery biscuits. There's also butter and jam. My brain still isn't functioning fully; I need a second cup of coffee. Steve picks up a tall glass of freshly squeezed orange juice that he special-ordered. We left the spa two weeks ago.

Yesterday we took an excursion to Cabo Polonio. In Europe Steve had heard about this little fishing village in Uruguay, so primitive that you have to pump your own water and light kerosene lanterns at night. Here everything is fragile and natural, and it's always full of sophisticated people who, naturally, want to get in touch with nature.

At two in the afternoon the bus arrives with its driver, a pleasant, serious Uruguayan who introduced himself by first and last names and shook everyone's hand. Repeating, "At your service," he collected our tickets and helped us climb aboard. And off we went through the green countryside, hillier than on this side of the river, looking at the trees alongside the road and a couple of cows in the distance, until we arrived at a very humble ranch; a faded, raggedy curtain poked out through a narrow window, waving in the breeze. But it was a farm, typical of the region, and that's why it was included as part of the excursion. We entered a grimy kitchen where there was a table covered in green oilcloth. We stood because there were only two chairs in the kitchen, one of them sturdy and the other rickety. In our group were two North Americans, a Belgian, and three Brazilians. No one spoke. The old woman made *mate* and passed it to the Belgian. I must express my admiration for those foreign tourists: they all tried the *mate*, at least one sip. They knew how to do it, and they didn't seem to care about the neglect and dubious cleanliness of the place. I, the only Latin American–River Plate sister, would rather have died than reject those folks' *mate*. But the only kind of *mate* I like is the kind with milk that they gave me when I was a kid. There's a scalloped photo of me that Mama took with the old box Kodak, sitting on a little chair with my personal *mate*-drinking equipment: tin sugar bowl and container for the leaves, tiny milk pitcher. You can see me in the photo sipping with great concentration, holding the *mate* gourd in both hands. It was a very sweet, lukewarm sort of *mate* that no one drinks anymore, least of all children today, who live on chocolate milk with cartoon characters.

There we were, Steve and I, he ever alert and interested in everything, I patiently enduring the inconveniences, until the old woman opened the oven door and placed an enormous tray of puff pastry with quince paste on the table. The best in the world, say the Uruguayans. They were still hot from the oven; they were delightful, and they made us very thirsty. The *mate* made the rounds again.

As we left the ranch, we saw a jeep parked in front of the bus. I knew that you could go to Cabo Polonio along the beach, in a jeep or by horse-drawn carriage. We took our belongings from the bus, and I patiently put up with the hard seats and jostling all the way back to Cabo Polonio. This thing that makes me join Steve even in his athletic feats, I thought, beginning with hang gliding, this thing that gives me pleasure just seeing how he enjoys it, must be love.

I thought it, but I didn't say it, because I need to make him believe I enjoy the adventure and because I'm a little ashamed to talk about love. At your age, Cecilia. When we arrived back in town, we climbed out of the jeep and began walking along the sand. I rubbed suntan lotion on my face and arms, and I passionately breathed the salty, iodine air that reminds me of countless vacations by the sea.

Every time I arrive at a beach, the memory of so many summer vacations comes back to me. There are also some I don't remember but which they told me about, showing me a little scalloped photo of myself on the sand. Mama insisted on going to the beach too early in the season; it was cold, and you had to breathe deeply. This is something they didn't tell me. I remember often having forced my lungs to breathe more air than necessary, on beaches or among the pines. Bathing was healthy, they said, although at times the water was very cold and the sky gray. But as you grow, you gain freedom, and later on they allowed me long walks along the shore, with the waves licking my feet.

Whenever I want to evoke a happy moment, I always see myself in a bathing suit, in the sun, bending down to pick up a snail, quickly digging a hole in order to pull out the clams that the waves wash in and which immediately hide in the sand. I was sixteen when we went to the old hotel at Mar del Sur, which used to be an insane asylum and before that a hotel for immigrants. The window in the room faced an enormous central patio with palm trees and benches; inside the nightstand I found a huge chamber pot. At a more modern hostelry two blocks from the hotel, like at the bar in San Conrado, there was dancing every night, especially to songs like "Cheek to Cheek" and "Mister Sandman":

Mister Sandman, bring me a dream,
Make her complexion like peaches and cream

My little children, sitting in the sand, on a piece of canvas from which they escaped every few minutes, a sandy ring invariably stuck around their tiny mouths.

We got out of the jeep and kept walking along the sand, sneakers in hand, until we reached the rocks.

I had already noticed that farther on the terrain became craggy, with very irregular rocks, but I assumed it was possible to cross over it and continue on the sand. And so I suddenly found myself trying not to be left behind, with my sneakers in my hand, because I saw that everyone else was removing theirs, concentrating on every step and with no time to decide which rock would best support my foot, that low, pointy one or the other one, flat but very high; from there you had to step on another stone some distance away, taking a bigger step, almost a leap; now I fall down and lose a few teeth; now I twist my ankle and nobody will want to wait for me, except Steve, of course, but what will the two of us do here all alone, me injured, between the desert and the sea? By the time the rocks ended and the sand began again, I was sweating, and the back of my neck hurt. No, Steve, I don't like sports.

My discomfort disappeared when we climbed up a sand dune to contemplate the vastness (how tiresome people are – they're happy only when they manage to contemplate vastness). Then, once more, the long row of beaches, waves, blue skies, the little shells and snails of so many summers of my life.

On the trip back, walking on the rocks didn't seem so awful to me. Lack of practice, I thought. How long had it been since I walked on rocks by the sea? When I was a girl, we used to have contests to see who could do more handstands on the beach – ten, fifteen, even twenty handstands, which left my hair full of sand. I always won. The bad part came later, in the hotel, when Mama made me take a bath and wash my hair even if there was no hot water.

"What are you thinking about, Cecilia?"

Steve's words come to me from another planet. I kiss him on the cheek without replying.

What was I thinking about? I wasn't thinking about Federico. I wasn't thinking about Dardo.

We rose from the table, left the hotel, and walked along the beach to the edge of the waves. Tomorrow we'll return to Buenos Aires.

ACKNOWLEDGMENTS

To François Couperin for the *Leçons de Ténèbres.*

To Georges Brassens for *Bonhomme.*

To Pablo Neruda for the phrase *Proudly poor.*

To Federico García Lorca and Lewis Carroll because it's always five in the afternoon.

To Aníbal Troilo because he didn't know if the neighborhood was like that.

To Lope de Vega because *the tears return.*

To Fernando Pessoa for
The poet is a fake.
His faking seems so real
That he will fake the ache
Which he can really feel.[3]

And:

To María Fasce for her excellent editing.

To the National Foundation of the Arts for the fellowship they awarded me in 1999 so that I could bring this book to fruition.

3. Fernando Pessoa, *Autopsychography*, trans. Keith Bosley.

Call Me Magdalena
By Alicia Steimberg
Translated by Andrea G. Labinger

The Rainforest
By Alicia Steimberg
Translated by Andrea G. Labinger

particular interest in women's writing, among them youth versus aging, marriage or domesticity versus career and self-realization, and conventional sexuality versus a greater sexual equality. Montero addresses a broad range of complex questions with maturity and insight."
—Janet Perez, author of *Ana María Matute*

ISBN: 0-8032-8183-8; 978-0-8032-8183-7 (paper)

Order online at www.nebraskapress.unl.edu or call 1-800-755-1105.
Mention the code "BOFOX" to receive a 20% discount.

University of Nebraska Press

Also of Interest in translation from Spanish:

Call Me Magdalena
By Alicia Steimberg
Translated by Andrea G. Labinger

Within the taut framework of a murder mystery, *Call Me Magdalena* moves through Magdalena's tortuous childhood as an Argentine Jew and through her doubts about morality and mortality, the existence of God, and the amorphous nature of identity.

ISBN: 0-8032-9282-1; 978-0-8032-9282-6 (paper)

A Broken Mirror
By Mercè Rodoreda
Translated and with an introduction by Josep Miquel Sobrer

A family saga extending from the prosperous Barcelona of the 1870s to the advent of the Franco dictatorship, *A Broken Mirror* shifts from one perspective to another, reflecting from myriad angles the founding of a matriarchal dynasty—and its eventual, seemingly inevitable disintegration.

ISBN: 0-8032-9007-1; 978-0-8032-9007-5 (paper)

The Delta Function
By Rosa Montero
Translated by Kari A. Easton and Yolanda Molina Gavilán

"First-rate, one of the major works by a woman in Spain during the last quarter-century. It treats many dualities of